BLOOD FATED

SHADOW PACK LEGENDS
BOOK FIVE

LUNA M. ROSE

PROLOGUE

Firelight flickered against stone walls, casting gold across the tangled linens beneath my thighs. I wasn't alone. His body lay beside mine, warm and smelling of salt and spice.

My mate.

My breath caught before I even understood why. Everything about this moment felt known. Whole. Like jasmine in full bloom.

He laughed low in his throat, the sound brushing against my skin like velvet. "You're staring again."

"Am I?"

He grinned without looking at me, dark lashes casting crescents over cheekbones bronzed from the sun. His hair fell in unruly waves to his jaw, and when he turned his face toward mine, it was like the air in my bed chamber turned to syrup. His smile was private. Just how I liked it.

He reached for me, fingers tracing my wrist. Up my arm, toying with the tender skin at the bend of my elbow. "You've been quiet tonight."

I swallowed, adjusting myself on the bed to expose more of myself. I wore only a dressing gown, and when it split open to reveal my chest, I didn't correct it.

He leaned in with a grin, lips grazing my collarbone. "You're thinking too much."

"I always think too much."

"Mmm." His mouth curved against my lips, his beard tickling my skin. "Then let me help." His hand slipped beneath the hem of the gown, callused fingertips dragging up the inside of my thigh. My legs parted without asking.

He kissed my neck. "If you're too tired, tell me to stop."

I arched into him as my fingers went to his waist, dragging his wrap loose. It fell in a whisper to the bed, and he was all golden skin and muscle, moonlight catching in the hollow of his throat. "I'll never tell you to stop. You know this."

He chuckled, his thumb brushing the amulet resting cold between my breasts. "The real question is, shall I leave this on or take it off with your gown?"

My laugh escaped before I could stop it. "When you gifted it to me, were you thinking of this very moment?"

He arched a brow. "Would you regret accepting it if that were true?"

I shook my head and reached for him again, slipping my arms from the sleeves of my gown. "Better?"

He hovered over me now, brushing a lock of hair from my face. "Much."

He bent to kiss me. Slowly. Deeply. His hand slid up, cupping my breast through thin fabric, and the heat between us sparked like flint. My back arched. My wolf stirred beneath my skin, more breath than body, watching through my eyes.

"I love you," he whispered against my mouth.

I smiled, and started to return the sentiment, but the

words wouldn't leave my lips. *I love you.* I wrestled with the phrase, trying to force it out between us. *I love you.*

His form began to fade above me, and I wrapped my arms around his back, gripping him with all the force in my body.

Don't go, I love you.

This was my choice. I knew it was. I hadn't told him, I hadn't held on tightly enough.

Please, stay with me. I love you.

I love you . . .

Erin

I shifted on the metal fold-out chair Rowan set up for me when I entered the shop. The back office at Steele Automotive was packed like a can of sardines. Evelyn sat on Rowan's lap in the office chair, not that she was complaining, Kael stood in the corner next to Callista, Lana and Destin perched on the edge of the desk, and my sister, Mia, and Connor sat on two chairs so close to mine, I had to keep my ankles crossed to avoid unintentional footsies.

"That's all we've got?" Rowan's voice was clipped.

Lana gave a sharp nod. She'd just finished detailing the disturbances around Kitimat and Black Lake that she and Destin had noticed over the past couple of weeks, but honestly, it was hard to take in the details. I could barely keep my eyes open, and the steady buzz from the overhead fluorescent light wasn't helping.

Mia tilted her head in my direction. "Connor and I can confirm. It's hard to describe, but there are traces of magic. Almost like a residue. We aren't sure yet what it means that they're so fresh, but we can feel it, too."

I kept my gaze trained on the forgotten metal washer on the carpet next to the leg of the desk. What was Mia trying to accomplish? Over the past week, she'd brought up her Shadow Realm discoveries more frequently than marathon runners flaunt their most recent PR's. Was she hoping it would tempt me? Act as bait? I hadn't expressed interest or desire to re-enter that damn place when we were alone, so what made her think I'd suddenly jump at the chance now?

"What do you need from us?" Evelyn asked.

Destin gave Lana a sidelong glance, then exhaled in a rush. "We need to hide the relics. We're not certain they're safe in the Shadow Realm, given the activity we're seeing."

Kael's jaw tensed. "You think the Northern Alphas know where they're hidden?"

Connor shrugged. "I straight up told them they were in the Shadow Realm."

"Right, but they don't have a way in, do they?" Evelyn asked.

"Theoretically, no." Lana tapped her fingers on the desk. "I'm not going to make that assumption, though."

"What does Gabriel say?" Mia asked.

I pursed my lips. *Gabriel.* That was Mia's answer to everything. He was a Shadow Pack warrior. He should know how to find the remaining relics and how to protect the ones we already had. The only problem was, none of us had seen him since that awkward bedside conversation in the Shadow Realm with Mia and Connor naked under their sheets.

Frustration lit a fire in my chest. I drew a deep breath and held it, that familiar bitterness bubbling up inside of me. It was like a wound that kept breaking open, and I couldn't figure out how to stop it.

You're bleeding all over the same floor again, my wolf growled. *Should've stayed gone.*

Fun. She was awake and raging again. When I first arrived home after the fire, my wolf all but disappeared. I thought that was disturbing enough, but this was worse. She'd never been like this. So hardened and bitter. I wasn't angry with my sister for coming after me, for reading my dreams, or for allowing Connor to take the bond that was mine. How could I be?

Easy, my wolf snapped.

I pressed my fingers harder against the mug, jaw tight. If anything, I was angry with myself. If I hadn't left—if I hadn't accepted James' offer—

If you hadn't trusted anyone. If you'd just listened to me. But no, she sneered, *you wanted to believe he was different. Charming, remember? Gentle with his lies. Just like Nathan.*

"Breathe."

I blinked, turning to see Mia hunched over Connor's lap. She stared at me with those honeyed eyes that mirrored mine. Nodding, I exhaled and refilled my lungs. This, me disappearing into my thoughts, was happening a lot lately.

One foot back in this place, and already they're touching us like they own us again.

She's trying to help, I told her. "Sorry," I murmured as Mia straightened, removing her hand. "What were you saying about Gabriel?"

Mia's brow arched. She knew how I felt about her hope that the warriors would come to save us. "He hasn't been available."

I fought back an eyeroll.

Lana ignored the distraction. "Here's what we know. The

relics seek each other, which makes them a tool for us to find the crown and the goblet, but since we know the goblet is in James' possession—"

"It's also a tool for him," Rowan finished.

"Exactly." Lana stood, crossing her arms over her chest. She looked like she wanted to pace, but there was no floor space.

"So we need to keep them safe," Callista mused. "But if magical traces are visible in the Shadow Realm—if the alpha's can get there—then what options do we have?"

"Not many." Lana's shoulders were so tense, they looked molded out of stone. She and Mia shared an ominous look. "But there is one."

Both of them turned to me, and my stomach dropped. *Shit.* "If this is another plan to get me into the Shadow Realm—"

"It's not," Mia assured me. "You don't have to go through to help with this, I promise."

My eyes narrowed. "Then why do you need me?"

It wasn't that I didn't want to be helpful, I did. But the idea of moving into the Shadow Realm made me queasy. Something about the dreams I was having, how they felt. It was too similar. Until I understood why I was seeing James's face in my subconscious—why it all felt so real—I wouldn't chance it.

The time I'd spent with James bonded to the amulet . . . it felt like a hundred years. The magic made my memories hazy, and I wanted to believe that was all this was. My brain was trying to recover the last six months and could only pull from the dark recesses of my mind while I was asleep.

But every time I soothed my inner voice with that line of reasoning, something hollow opened up in my middle. *It wasn't the same. I'd never seen him like that before.* Something inside me knew the images in my head were different.

Of course it's different. My wolf sounded more tired than

angry now. *But please, sit back while another alpha abuses his power.*

I shivered, trying to block her out. The pack leaders talked of magical traces and connections between the relics while I fought the strange pull below my ribcage that flared every time I went to sleep. I *was* helping them by staying put. Flying under the radar. They just didn't know it.

Yes, I could've said something, brought up my concerns, but Mia was already hovering over me like a mother hen, and none of them would have answers that I didn't. Except maybe Gabriel, wherever the hell he was.

Lana started, "We're not sure exactly how it works, but there's something connected to dreams—"

"Absolutely not." I shook my head, panic rising in my throat.

"Hear her out," Mia pleaded.

"I don't need to." I turned to my sister, my hands already clenched, my breathing quickening. "I told you what I see there. It's bad enough that I can't escape when I sleep—"

"But maybe there's a reason." Mia's eyes flashed. "Maybe you were born with exactly what you need to help rebuild the Shadow Pack, Erin. I get that it's scary—"

"No, you *don't* get it." I pushed up from my chair, the metal legs scraping against the linoleum. The room spun, and sweat broke out on my forehead.

Mia groaned. "Erin—"

I threaded through the others, making my way to the door. Not exactly a dramatic exit when I needed to do a full-on obstacle course before rushing out.

To her credit, Mia didn't try to physically stop me. I stumbled through the busy garage, trying not to catch the attention of any of Rowan's guys under the hoods. Many of them were people I'd grown up with. It was a strange feeling—being home, but not really home. Here, my home had always been my family, my pack. That safety was blown apart when Nathan took over, which meant everything should've felt normal now. Black Lake and Kitimat were blended, and Nathan Black was gone. Still. Nothing felt the same.

It was like a switch had been flipped off inside of me the day Nathan appeared at our door, and I couldn't figure out how to flip it back on. Possibly because there were still three alphas out there reminding me that I wasn't in a safe haven here. Packs were supposed to be a refuge. But if my dreams were to be believed, it didn't seem possible for me to shelter anymore. What pack could protect me from my own head?

My wolf didn't even have to say anything.

I pushed through the doors into the parking lot and realized instantly that I'd left my coat back in Rowan's office. I shivered at the blast of cold air and hurried to my car. Even though I wasn't excited about winter approaching, I couldn't complain about the clear blue sky and crisp, clean air. After living in a cloud of smoke for the past couple of months, it was something I would never take for granted again.

I slipped into the passenger seat of Connor's truck, wishing I had declined their invitation to ride over together. As I'd so gracefully proclaimed in the garage, Mia didn't understand this. It wasn't her fault. It's not like I was doing anything to let her in, but how could I, when she seemed so blissfully happy?

She had Connor, and I was glad for that. Besides my sister, the only relationship I had was with the lone wolves I'd abandoned to follow James. I'd burned bridges with my family and then torched the ones with my friends. It was better for everyone if I stayed unattached.

Shame curled at the base of my spine, knowing that every single one of the shifters in that office had risked their lives to save mine. Ironic that my memories of that day were still crystal clear. The image of Connor slashing his skin. Of Kael standing within a torrent of flame. *They were okay,* I reminded myself. *My sister was okay.*

But every time I drove the stretch of highway north of Kitimat and saw the blackened trees in the distance, I was reminded who had paid that debt.

The amulet had given James immeasurable power and allowed him to access a dark well that none of us fully understood. Ironically, that was one of the only tethers that kept me from packing up the hatchback I'd purchased by scraping the dregs from my savings account and leaving British Columbia. We didn't understand that dark magic, but so many of us had felt it.

While Mia and Connor were still stranded in the Shadow Realm, Kael and Lana had sought me out independently. Both of them had felt the pull of the dagger. And Lana knew the call of the book. But the amulet was something wholly different. And the difference was? I hadn't been strong enough to pull myself out of it.

Connor had done that for me.

I wondered if that was why I still felt its echoes—because it hadn't been my choice. Because part of me still yearned for that power. Lana had the amulet, and Connor had absorbed the bond, nearly dying in the process. Mia had sacrificed herself to save him. That was supposed to be enough to neutralize whatever thirst the amulet had. It had worked with the dagger.

So why was I still feeling that pull? Why was I seeing James?

The driver's side door opened, and I jumped, then frowned as Mia popped up into the driver's seat.

"Where's Connor?" I asked.

Mia pressed the start button. "He's helping Rowan with a project."

That was code for "I wanted to talk to you alone," and we both knew it. She reversed out of the parking spot, then put the truck in drive and headed for the street.

"Talk to me, Erin." Mia's hands clenched the wheel.

"I have talked to you. I've told you everything I've seen." That was true. The only things I'd left out were feelings, a few instances of a voice I'd heard but didn't know who it belonged to. None of that was relevant.

Mia blew out a resigned breath. "I might be able to do it."

"Do what?" I frowned.

"Access the magic needed to hide the relics."

My frown deepened. "Lana said it required dreaming."

"I know. And if you remember, I can access that through you."

My voice hardened. "Mia, I already said no."

"Will you please just hear me out? You wouldn't even have to be dreaming for me to try. I've accessed those things when you've been fully awake, if you remember."

Something fluttered low in my belly. Yeah. I remembered. It was the summer I turned twelve. I'd been sitting on the back porch reading a book, minding my own business, when Mia came out and tried to get me to walk with her to the park. She yanked on me, nearly pulling me off the camping chair when she stopped.

Her head flew up, her mouth dropped open. A few seconds later, she blinked and dropped my arm. "You kissed Liam?"

My eyes flew wide. "What? No! I—"

"I saw it! In your head!"

. . .

I NEARLY DIED RIGHT THERE on the steps. I'd had the dream the night before, and it hadn't even been that bad. Just us messing around in the woods and then . . . yeah. A kiss.

Mia smirked. "Have you talked with Liam since coming back?"

"Ew, no." I crossed my arms over my chest like I was twelve again.

Mia laughed out loud. We drove in silence for a few moments.

"Lana mentioned a place." Mia turned off the main road. "If you had stayed for another few minutes, you would've heard that part." She shot me a look. "But, yes, as we've studied the traces we were mentioning, we noticed a strange void. We've found two so far. Almost like a black hole, which I know sounds ridiculous because I do understand what a black hole is, but I can't figure out how else to describe it. It's like there's a tear or a ripple of nothingness. Lana searched the book, and it talked about dreamwalkers—"

"If this is another thing you're going to tell me I've ruined—"

"No. I don't think it's caused by that." She paused, wetting her lips. "Well, I don't know. Maybe it is, but it described a method for sealing it up. And it requires a dream to do that. It requires someone to be in both places at once. Can you think of any other way that would happen? Except through a dream?"

I opened my mouth and closed it again. That was exactly how it felt when James was there in my head. Both places at once.

Mia pulled into the parking lot of my apartment complex. I'd lived with her and Connor for all of three days before realizing there was no way in hell that would work. She put the truck in park.

"Will you come with me and just let me try? You can be fully awake."

I leaned my head back on the headrest. "Mia, it's not about being awake or asleep. I don't want to access that power ever."

"Because of what you remember and what you see?"

I nodded, allowing her to believe that was the extent of it. Mia slumped over the wheel, dropping her forehead onto her hands. "I don't want to ask this of you, Erin, but if we can't secure those relics, I don't think you're just going to be seeing James in your dreams. He's going to be here, or he's going to find us in the Shadow Realm."

My eyes burned. I didn't want to disappoint her any more than I already had. It was the only reason I opened my mouth and said, "But what if this connection I feel isn't only one-sided?"

Mia stilled and, a moment later, lifted her head to look at me. "You think he can see you, too?"

I shrugged. "I don't know. But I can't figure out why he would be in my head. What if by using that power, I'm giving him exactly what he wants?"

Mia nodded slowly. "The location of the relics."

Understanding flickered in her eyes. Why I resisted going to meetings. Why I didn't want to talk about any of their plans. Again, it wasn't the whole truth. I still couldn't put into words the other things I'd felt there.

Truthfully, my whole life I'd felt some deep sense of regret, like I always owed an apology. I didn't want to make any more mistakes, and that meant I threw my entire soul into the things I believed in. When I found out what was happening in feedlots, I switched to only eating meat from local small farms or opting out and eating vegetarian. My parents loved that.

When I discovered the clothes I purchased were made in sweatshops overseas, I switched to thrifting. To this day, I only bought my clothes second-hand. It wasn't a perfect solution, but it was the best I could do on a limited budget.

I didn't want to be the source of more pain. I didn't want to mess anything else up.

Mia blew out a breath. "That's a good point. I'll talk to the others, see if they think the risk is worth it."

I nodded and reached for the door handle, then stopped when Mia's hand wrapped around my arm, holding me back.

"I'm worried about you, Erin. I know coming home can't be easy. I might not get it, but there are people who understand. Evelyn left and came back. She was hurt by Nathan, too, and Callista—"

"I know." I repressed the shiver starting at the top of my spine. Both Evelyn and Callista had offered to talk. And while our stories did have similarities, there was one major piece missing from theirs.

I had chosen it. I chose to accept what James offered. I chose to connect with the relic. They had been victims, but I? I had willingly jumped in. That whole soul full speed ahead thing wasn't exactly working out well for me in this situation.

"I'll think about it." I waited for her hand to drop, then got out of the truck and walked up the stairs to my apartment.

I wasn't going to think about it. The only thing I was pondering at the moment was how the hell I could break whatever connection I had with James and the amulet that he and I seemed to share. Anything I did, any meeting I attended, any conversation I participated in, was me hunting for clues. *There had to be something I was missing, and I needed to fix this.*

I locked the deadbolt and dropped my purse on the couch, then flicked on the TV to old reruns of "Law and Order" before hunting in the refrigerator for anything I could make for an early dinner.

I couldn't sit down, due to the very real possibility I would nod off, and I needed to wait. I needed to wait until at least seven when I could take a sleeping pill. That was the only thing that dropped me deep enough to give me the highest chance of escaping the night without dreams.

I pulled open the vegetable drawer to find a cucumber and two lemons, then rummaged for the cheese and salami. I took my time eating over the next hour, trying to recall if I knew the episode's ending. The one where the twelve-year-old's father was found dead. I swear I'd seen it before, but the familiar story pattern was comfortable.

I realized it wasn't exactly healthy for me to stay cooped up in my apartment, living on charcuterie. But the idea of being social made me want to come down with the flu. Or measles, since that was apparently going around. Not that I would actually catch any of that. Straight-up humans had it so easy when it came to physical malady scapegoats.

I brushed my teeth and washed my face, taking in my appearance in the mirror. I'd kept my hair pulled back for days. It was just long enough to fit into a small looped bun at the base of my skull. I pulled out the elastic and shook it out. It was more of a mousy brown now since I'd spent so little time out in the sun. The face looking back seemed older than the one I knew—shadows under my green eyes, a mouth too serious for someone my age.

I downed my sleeping pill with enough water that I wouldn't choke, but not so much that I'd wake up groggily trying to make my way to the bathroom at four in the morning. This was the best part of my day. Not the actual blacking out, but the anticipation of it, knowing that in approximately twenty-three minutes, I would hopefully get actual rest. After my mind wandered for a bit, the drug took effect, and my thoughts got that distant, ethereal quality about them. Like they were somehow farther away from my head.

With a sigh of relief, I allowed it to take me under. When I blinked my eyes open, the world was still dark. I could barely make out the faint lines of my doorway. Wait. *Was it a doorway?* The lines weren't perfectly straight.

I rubbed my eyes, recognizing at once that I wasn't lying down. I was standing on soft ground. "Shit," I hissed under my breath. *Not in my bed.* And that could only mean one thing.

CHAPTER
TWO

ERIN

A shimmer pulsed at the edge of my vision. I turned, but the world moved with me, as if I were standing in the reflection of a pond.

A stone corridor. Vaulted ceilings. Something between cathedral and crypt.

I stumbled back, trying to find some kind of cover. James and the other two alphas had never looked at me in this realm. They'd never shown any indication that they knew I was there. But *he* had—whoever he was.

I felt him every single time I entered here, heard him only sometimes, and never once had I laid eyes on him. It was as if he were part of the atmosphere. Part of my own head. Maybe that was the easiest explanation—that I was going insane.

We didn't have any data on the relics to prove otherwise.

Maybe being under the influence of the amulet for that long had addled my neurons or something. Maybe that was why.

He'd never hurt me. If anything, it seemed like he was just as interested in helping me stay under James's radar as I was. That's where it didn't make sense. I was already being careful. Why would my brain conjure up some other person to keep me safe? Especially when knowing that I wasn't alone only brought me more anxiety.

Voices lifted in the distance. This realm was so strange. I could never flesh out how close sounds or objects were to me. I folded into myself, trying to make every piece of myself smaller.

Wake up. It was a futile command. I'd taken the sleeping pill, so I was out cold for at least a few hours. Pangs of nausea hit the dream version of myself.

"If you can feel it, why don't I have it?" a voice growled, the words crystal clear.

I winced. It was James's voice. I knew it well by now.

I slid to the ground, pulling my knees to my chest and pressing my fingers to both of my temples.

"It's not that simple," another voice snapped. Didn't recognize that one. Fantastic. There were more than three of them now.

Focus.

If I had to be here, at least I could try and learn something to take back to Lana. But who knew if this was even real? If anything I saw here was helpful, it was only bits and pieces, and trying to derive any meaning from it was pointless.

Goosebumps rose on my skin as a breeze whispered featherlight over the backs of my arms.

Not a breeze.

I understood that by now, too.

He was here.

Him—it?—I had no idea since I'd never caught sight of the owner of the voice in my head.

I set my jaw. Would I hear him tonight? Or would I sit there for hours as shivers passed over my neck and down my spine as usual?

"Move."

A mixture of relief and dread twisted through me at the rough command. I turned my head, but just as always, there was nothing to be seen. He was invisible. Or fast. Or he didn't have a physical form.

I huffed, wishing I could ignore it or command him in return—demand he show himself—but I'd tried all of that already. If I didn't do as he said, I would find myself wrapped in bands of shadow and compelled anyway.

I blinked as a thought flashed in my head.

The amulet.

The compulsion.

That's how it had felt, hadn't it? Was that what this was?

Lana had said the relics were becoming more volatile, calling to each other. Its hold on me had broken when Connor used the dagger. But was there still a lingering connection there?

Was that why I was pulled here? And was that the voice I heard? *Could it be the relic speaking?*

I scrambled up from the ground and hissed, "Where?"

A breath of air, a nudge to my left as James's voice cracked through the space behind me.

"My patience is wearing thin."

Had he really just said that? It was almost comical. Such a classic villain line.

I crept forward, obedient to the pressure against the right side of my body. If this was some strange reaction to the amulet's power, would James feel it too? Is that why Lana was so worried? I would probably know the answer to that if I'd been willing to talk to her.

The air constricted around me, hustling me along. "Impatient," I murmured. If it was the relic toying with me, I doubted I could cause any more harm by talking back.

"You should not be here."

"So you keep telling me."

"Have you done nothing to shield your mind?"

I exhaled, closing my eyes and allowing the force to take me fully. There was no point fighting it. "You say that as if it's obvious how I could accomplish that."

"Your mind is weak."

"Thank you." Again, nothing new. Another reason why I hated coming here, and probably one of the red flags that I was making this shit up all on my own. Insisting I was both wrong and embarrassingly weak was one of my subconscious's favorite pastimes.

I gasped as we came to an instant stop. "What—" I started to say when my mouth was sealed shut.

"I feel it." A voice sounded on my right. The same voice that had been talking with James.

I forced air through my nostrils, panic setting in.

"It's been here before, but not this strong."

Blood rushed in my ears. Nobody had any doubt that James was hunting for the relics, but what was this I was seeing? Was it happening now, or was it something I'd witnessed during his hunt for the book? For the dagger?

My heart sped, threatening to choke me. If I did still have a connection to the amulet, could they sense me here? Did the amulet not want to be found by him? Was that why I was always being hustled away? Told to leave?

Did the relics have a preference for who wielded them?

I turned my head in the direction of the voice, and the breath whooshed out of my lungs.

James stood ten paces away with a man I didn't recognize.

Both of them stared directly at me.

James looked exactly as I remembered. Tall with his barrel chest and wavy dark hair. Even from here, his blue eyes cut like glass. The other, though . . . he was unfamiliar. Stockier, his hair buzzed until his scalp was nearly bald, a cold sneer on his lips.

I fell back instinctively, but the bands around me tightened, holding me in place. Not arms, just sensation. Pressure and heat and the sharp, dizzying prickle of lightning across my skin. It was tight, but comfortable. Like I was being swaddled.

James and his friend peered at me in the dark, then stalked closer. My breaths became shallow as I fought to free myself, but my limbs were frozen in place.

"Shh." The whisper hummed in my ear. I didn't dare beg like I wanted to, but I couldn't force myself to stop struggling. What the hell was happening? Why hide me in every dream prior, then present me like a lamb to the slaughter?

James stopped in front of me, his head cocking slightly. "It's here." His voice—so familiar, so utterly wrong—scraped across my already live-wire nerves.

My heart galloped, and the warmth behind me responded, curling tighter around my waist.

They could see me. I knew it. James's gaze was locked forward, piercing, endless. My lungs forgot how to inflate. But then the second man moved closer, and his eyes seemed unfocused. Like he was looking through me, not at me.

"Too close," the silver-eyed man said. "Their pattern loops through the wood, through town, and back again. The dagger was in the river. I could taste it."

James's mouth curled. "Let them play their games. Their creativity will eventually become predictable. It always does."

My chest pinched. The river. Had the dagger been there before when Lana held it? Was this a memory resurfacing? Had I met this man before and didn't remember?

"And if she enters?" the second man asked.

James scoffed. "She won't." He turned on his heel and took two steps before pausing and turning back. His brow twitched.

"You're so certain?"

James wet his lips. "She's too eager to see me again. It shames her."

My eyes flew wide. *Not you!* I wanted to scream, but my lips were once again sealed shut. *The amulet! Not you!*

James turned and continued on his path down the stone hall, and the other man followed. Once they disappeared around the corner, my mouth fell open with a guttural sob.

Me. He'd been talking about me. Those words cut to my core, flayed me open, and I wanted to bury myself beneath the stone—anything to purge the oily film spreading through me.

"It calls to him, too," the deep voice murmured as I lowered to my knees, the bands still refusing to let me go.

"Don't try to comfort me." I wiped my nose with my sleeve, tears clouding my vision.

"You can't stop—"

"I don't want it!" I pressed my palms into the stone, heaving for breath. "I hate that damn necklace, and I don't ever want to see it again!"

My voice echoed off the stone, and my head snapped up. If they heard, if they came back, what would James do to me? What could he see? Take?

My heart thundered against the pressure at my back. "They know," I whispered. "They *sensed* me—"

"They sensed the relics," the presence corrected. A brush of breath at my temple. "You are part of them now, and they are a part of you."

The words themselves didn't make me think of Mia's question in the truck, but somehow I *felt* the suggestion. It made sense in the way only dreams do—in a way that would fade and seem silly once I woke.

I shook my head, throat raw. "I can't purposefully access this power. I can't bring a relic into this realm. They can sense my presence! I'll lead them straight to everything we're trying to protect."

"I was wrong, then."

I drew in my first full breath. "Wrong about what?"

"I thought you weren't still under his command."

My eyes flared. "You're being unfair."

"And you're being stubborn."

"Am I?"

Silence. For a moment, I wondered if he'd gone, but pressure still wrapped around my shoulders, my waist.

When he spoke again, his voice was low and rough. "James doesn't expect you to return."

I pushed up to my knees, my hands and arms trembling. "For good reason."

"Fear is never a good reason," he snapped.

That sentence sank into me like rain on parched ground. The bands loosened, and something traced a line from my elbow to my wrist. My breath shivered past my lips, my head tilting back before I could stop it.

And then he was gone.

I kneeled alone on the stone, my tears drying on my cheeks.

CHAPTER

THREE

The veil snapped closed behind me, the dream dissolving in my wake. I stood at the edge of the nothing between realms, breath shallow. Her voice still clung to me.

Am I?

Two words that cracked something open inside me. Opened a door that I thought I'd sealed shut a thousand years ago.

I forced my hands to still, fingers curling into fists to stop the trembling. The wound she'd pressed had no right to still ache. And yet it burned hot in the marrow of me.

I turned and began to walk, the landscape blurring around me. The Shadow Realm was silent, but I knew better than to think that was because it was empty. Someone was always watching here.

A shape shimmered before me. A ruined hall long buried beneath time. I didn't summon it, but the realm didn't need a command to bring us what we wanted. Sometimes it liked to wound me with its own remembering.

Once, this place had been our stronghold. The high court of the Kainos shifters. Pillars carved with sacred trees. Tapestries woven with the symbols of earth and bone.

Skin like summer stone, hair soaked in starlight. Wasn't that what I'd written to her? We weren't supposed to be lovers. Warriors bore oaths, not hearts. And yet when the wolves ruled the north, when our bloodlines still held honor and the sacred bore weight, I had been hers.

She'd worn the amulet James sought. The one he'd forced around Erin's neck. I'd barely been able to look at it.

And now those two words . . .

The memory threatened to flood me. I worked to push it back. To swallow it like a blade, but it wouldn't be tamped down.

She was watching me.

I didn't need to look to know it. I could feel her gaze like sunlight. It slid over the slope of my shoulder, across the scars I never let others see, down to the place where her name lived just beneath my ribs.

"You're staring again."

"Am I?" she said, her voice low and half-daring.

I let the corner of my mouth curl as I turned toward her. Her bed chamber glowed with the heat of midsummer, though the sun had long slept, the linen sheets kicked to the edge of the mattress.

I reached for her. She didn't flinch. Gods, she never did.

My hand skimmed the soft skin of her wrist, followed the pale inner curve of her arm up to the delicate hollow of her elbow. She was gowned in silk that clung and parted like it had been made to fall off for me.

"You've been quiet," I murmured.

She shifted, her thigh brushing mine, and the robe gaped lower across her chest. The sight stole a beat from my heart.

I leaned in slowly, brushing my mouth against her collarbone. Her skin smelled like lavender and the wind off the cliffs. The taste of her lived on my tongue. "You're thinking too much."

"I always think too much."

"Mmm." My lips curved against her skin. The softness of her. The hum beneath. The way her pulse ticked steadily beneath the weight of my mouth.

"Then let me help."

"NO!" I raged into the darkness, gasping for breath. *No.* I would not relive that night.

I had watched the first of the relics be forged. The crown. The goblet. The book. The dagger. Four pieces of a promise and a fifth, I hadn't spoken of until I was awoken.

A relic born in blood.

I'd stood watch as they carved the runes into the dagger's hilt, sealing shadow into steel. I'd held her when she wept after binding the book's spine with a piece of her own soul. I'd kissed her neck before she left her bed chamber that final night.

And I'd told her we could bear the price.

I was wrong.

When my consciousness finally tore free of its stone prison, I dressed in the dark. *It was my fault. All of this was my fault.* Shirt. Hoodie. Jeans. Shoelaces knotted with shaking fingers as I berated myself for not buying the Birkenstocks I'd seen on sale at Murphy's last weekend.

The shadows of the dream clung to me like smoke. Fear is never a good reason. I kept replaying those words, and they stung like a splinter under my skin, just deep enough to hurt when I breathed.

My fingertips hesitated over the edge of my dresser. I waited for my stomach to right itself, then grabbed my keys and shoved them into my pocket. I hadn't felt this kind of dread since the night Nathan Black nearly killed my mother.

The sound of his boots on our living room floor would never leave my head. The slam of a door. The wet, sick crack when his hand collided with her cheekbone.

It hadn't been a question then. The injustice, I couldn't abide it. I had to leave—had to run. The same instinct pulled at me now, insisting I walk out of my apartment and make my way north. But this was different. No amount of travel was going to distance me from what I found in the dark.

The air outside bit at my skin. Dawn hadn't quite broken yet. There were just bruised clouds and the faintest suggestion of gold on the horizon. I slammed the door and locked it, then made my way to the stairs.

Everything smelled like frost and damp concrete mixed with the occasional waft of pine smoke from someone's wood-stove. Seemed I wasn't the only one up at this miserable hour. My apartment building—a slab of gray stucco with brick accents—was dark except for the occasional porchlight. Thankfully, there were a few streetlights illuminating the side-walk as I jogged up the street. I wasn't normally afraid of being outside at night, but the idea of "normal" at this point was lunacy.

A raccoon darted across a side street, nearly giving me a heart attack, but by the time I reached the highway, I'd settled into a rhythm. Sharp breath in. Slow breath out. One foot, then the other.

I should've called Mia and had her come pick me up, but honestly, it never occurred to me. Possibly because I needed to move, to try and metabolize the adrenaline already coursing through me.

The sky lightened fractionally. That pre-dawn hour when everything turned blue and hollow. Cold clung to my wrists. I shoved my hands into my hoodie and nearly missed the low growl of tires behind me.

A pickup slowed, and my heart kicked into high gear. Was this just my life now? Did I have a sign over my head blinking, "Hey! I'm vulnerable! Please take advantage of me!"

I picked up my pace as a voice sounded behind me.

"Erin?"

I tripped on a branch and caught myself.

"Erin, stop."

The truck door slammed, and I turned to see Liam jogging along the shoulder. His dark hair was still tousled from sleep, eyes wide under the brim of a backwards ball cap. He wore a t-shirt like he'd blacked out and forgotten the temperature.

"What the hell are you doing?" He slowed and shoved his hands in the pockets of his jeans.

I gestured at the street. "What does it look like?"

"Uh . . . like you murdered someone and buried the body. Now you're hitchhiking out of town."

I laughed in spite of myself. "You offering a getaway car?"

"Obviously." He nodded toward the truck.

Part of me wanted to decline and continue along the road, but the traffic was going to heat up now that the sun was rising, and I still had at least two kilometers to go before turning off on Cherry Creek to climb the hill to Mia's.

I exhaled and strode into the high beams. Liam didn't ask any questions once we were inside the cab. He reached over and turned the heat up. The cab smelled faintly of gas station coffee and pine air freshener.

"New truck?" I asked.

The corner of his mouth curled as he pulled out onto the highway. "Yeah."

"It's nice."

"I've been saving up for a while." He drummed his fingers once on the steering wheel. "You're getting the full tour. Heat, seat warmers, tunes if you want them. This thing's got all the bells and whistles."

I glanced around the interior. The leather felt and smelled brand new. "When did you get it?"

"Last week. Finally traded in the Ford. She was on her last leg. Literally. Rear axle was going."

"That truck was older than you."

"Practically born in it." He grinned, and despite everything, the corner of my mouth twitched.

Everyone in Kitimat knew the story. Liam's mom had nearly given birth to him in the back seat of that rusted-out beast during a freak snowstorm. She'd gone into labor three weeks early while hauling firewood across the east ridge, too stubborn to call for help until it was almost too late. My father and two others had loaded her into the truck while a blizzard rolled down the mountain, and they'd driven blind for twenty miles over ice-thick roads.

They barely made it to the midwife, parked the truck, and had her waddling to the front door when she dropped right there on the step. Liam arrived fast. First breath and first cry that the elders swore had shaken every window for miles.

He'd shifted twice before he could walk. First in the crib. Then again when he was three, because another kid pushed Mia too hard at the riverbank.

Some pups came into their power with a whisper. Liam burst into the world already halfway wild. And somehow, he'd always stayed soft around the edges.

I thought of that dream kiss and shuddered. He was younger than me then. Still was, in fact. His hands relaxed on the wheel as his gaze flicked toward the turnoff to Mia and Connor's without asking if that's where we were headed.

Liam flicked his turn signal on. "Doubt she'll be up by now."

I wondered how he felt about everything that had happened up north. About Mia and Connor. Somehow, I'd always thought Liam and my sister would end up together.

We pulled onto the gravel road leading up to Mia and Connor's. Morning mist curled along the edges of the ditches, gold beginning to burn through the fog.

I sighed. "Yeah."

He waited until we pulled into the driveway, then parked and cleared his throat. "Must be pretty important."

I gripped the edge of the seat. With the relics pulling closer together and the power the Northern Alphas were able to wield, there was no doubt that our protections would weaken.

It had already started, according to Rowan. Quietly. Subtly. Ward lines flickering. Old barriers going fuzzy at the edges like someone had smudged them with their fingers. Rowan said it was a flux. Lana said it was temporary. But deep down, every one of us knew what it meant.

Shifters weren't just made to survive the dark—we were built to hold the line against it. That was the point of all of it. The teeth. The instincts. The pack bond. The rituals and the long nights spent walking fence lines soaked in foxglove and ash root. We were the wall between the normal world and everything it didn't want to believe in. Now we were holding that wall together with grit and guesswork. If the protections kept failing, then the dark things we were meant to keep out wouldn't need to knock. They'd just walk in.

I glanced sideways at Liam. He'd seen everything up north, but since returning to Black Lake, he'd been working with Tori, helping with rotations and perimeter security. It had to be killing him that Lana and Rowan were keeping things so close to the chest—that he wasn't around to be a part of the group.

Liam exhaled. "You want me to come with?"

I shook my head.

"Didn't think so." There was no offense in his voice. Just truth.

My fingers hovered over the door handle. "Thanks, Liam."

He shrugged. "What are getaway cars for?"

I gave a small smile, then dropped to the ground. Gravel crunched under my shoes as I climbed the steps and rapped my knuckles on the front door. The knock felt too loud in the quiet. I stepped back and wrapped my arms around myself, bracing against the wind sneaking down the back of my hoodie.

Behind me, Liam's truck paused just long enough to see the porch light flick on. Then his reverse lights blinked, and he eased down the drive.

The deadbolt clicked. The door cracked open with a creak like old bones. Mia blinked out at me, her face half-shadowed, her curls a wild halo of sleep. She wore a hoodie that had definitely once belonged to Connor, sleeves bunched at her wrists, and her socks didn't match.

For a second, she just stared. Then her eyes sharpened. "Erin?"

I nodded, and she opened the door wider. The warmth hit like a solid wall as I pulled the storm door open and stepped into the entryway.

Behind Mia, Connor emerged shirtless, sleep-creased, barefoot in black pajama pants slung low on his hips. Muscles coiled under golden skin, and a faint pink scar tracked up his left side. I would've gawked had my eyes not snagged on the tire iron clutched in his hands.

My eyes widened.

His shoulders dropped as he lowered the weapon to his side. "Couldn't smell you." He nodded at me once and ducked into the kitchen. A moment later, I heard the soft clatter of mugs.

Mia's hand found my arm. "Come sit. You want food, or—no, coffee first." She steered me toward the couch like I was made of thin glass.

I sat down. A throw blanket rested on the edge of the couch, and I pulled it over my lap, not bothering to pretend I wasn't shaking. We sat there in silence for what seemed like ten minutes. It was probably only three.

Mia disappeared into the kitchen and returned with two steaming mugs. She handed me one before perching on the coffee table in front of me, hands wrapped around her own cup. "What happened?"

The pack bond I'd been working to silence lit up. Mia was the one saying the words, but she'd alerted the others that I was here. They'd all be listening.

I stared into the coffee. The surface trembled, tiny rings rippling out toward the rim. "You were right. The alphas are tracking us. Well, they're tracking the relics," I said finally. My voice came out hoarse. "I saw James in my dream. They're following everything from the Shadow Realm."

Mia didn't move, but her spine tightened. Her fingers whitened around the mug. "Connor," she said without turning.

"Yep. On it," came his voice from the kitchen.

Mia looked me in the eye. "You dreamt this?"

I nodded.

Mia didn't say another word, just rose and returned a moment later with a thicker blanket from the hall linen closet. It smelled like the kind of detergent you can only get from tiny, overpriced health stores. She tucked it around me like I was a kid again.

I took a sip of my coffee now that it was cool enough to ingest. Burnt, slightly bitter, perfect.

Mia sat beside me this time, shoulder to shoulder. "The others will be here soon."

"Mm." It was all I could say, considering my wolf was full-on gnashing her teeth. *Chill!* I barked in my head. *I don't like this either, but it's not like I can disappear again with James sniffing them out.*

She growled, pawing with her head lowered and ears flat. I wasn't a patron saint by sitting here on Mia's couch. I was desperate. *We both are,* I hissed, and that seemed to shut her up for the moment.

By the time the first knock came, the sun had dragged itself fully above the horizon. Light cut through the treetops in thin golden shards, turning the mist into something out of a dream —or a warning. The kind of morning that meant *change.*

Connor opened the door, and Kael stepped through first, eyes sharp, his jacket half-zipped and wind in his hair. Callista followed, a thermos in one hand and an entire gallon of milk in the other. Hadn't caught that request over the pack bond.

Rowan was next, dark brows drawn, jaw already locked into battle mode. He glanced at me, and his expression softened a degree before he turned back to Connor. Lana and Destin brought up the rear, looking like they hadn't slept. Destin's eyes locked on mine for a long beat.

"No Evelyn?" Lana asked.

Rowan shook his head. "She's going to stay with the others."

"Probably smart." Lana turned, and I moved to the table so I wouldn't get stuck standing in the spotlight. Mia followed with the coffee pot and enough mugs to keep us functional. They made small talk, joked with each other in low voices. When the conversation petered out, I knew I couldn't avoid this any longer.

I took a breath. Then another. "You heard what I told Mia."

Lana's brows knitted. "Not surprising. We knew the goblet would try to reunite with the others."

My throat tightened. *You're part of them.* What did the voice in my dreams mean by that? Was I a liability like I thought? Could James and the other alphas sense me? *Could Lana sense me?*

The question teetered on the tip of my tongue, but I swallowed it down. "He's got someone with him. A man. I don't know who he is."

Callista exchanged a glance with Kael, but neither spoke.

Destin leaned forward, his arm protectively wrapped around Lana. "Are they here, in the physical world? Or only spying from the Shadow Realm?"

I hesitated. The idea of James camping in the hills made me want to dry heave.

Lana blew out a breath. "They think the relics are in the Shadow Realm. But that doesn't mean they won't look everywhere."

"And if we find the last relic . . ." Rowan let that thought hang in the air.

The magic would only increase. I wasn't sure how close they were to discovering a lead on the crown, but we knew where the goblet was. Theoretically. What would happen if James brought that near the others?

A thought clicked in my head. Would James be in that strange space where we kept meeting? Could he access it like I could, or was he in the Shadow Realm and I was somehow seeing through?

Maybe he wouldn't be there. Maybe he'd feel the same pull from the Shadow Realm but wouldn't know where to look. Mia said I didn't have to go through, and I believed her. Dream walking wasn't the same. The problem was, I didn't know what it was. Nobody really did.

"I'll try. To seal them," I said. They all looked at me, surprise flickering in their eyes. "I'll do it myself."

Mia's eyes widened. *That's a big sacrifice,* she sent through the bond.

Guilt twisted between my ribs. Not that big. I couldn't risk being found by James or being controlled by this connection with the amulet. If I sealed it up, maybe that would buy me some time to figure out how to extricate myself. It was a win-win, wasn't it?

Find him. I'll tear his throat out, my wolf snarled. A very timely contribution.

Where were you with that promise last night? I asked.

She huffed and paced in my head. I understood perfectly. The rage I felt toward Nathan Black, toward James, wasn't enough to force myself up off the floor to do anything in the moment.

"We should move." Lana brushed off Destin's arm and stood. "The sooner, the better."

FIVE

Erin

Lana led us to an old logging trail an hour past the edge of town. The road wasn't on any map I knew of. Roots split the ground like veins, and our trucks barely had the clearance to avoid bottoming out.

We stopped where the trees arched overhead. Lana was the first to get out of the truck, and the rest of us followed. The air didn't move. No wind. No birdsong.

"This is it." Lana scuffed her boot across the mulch. "This is where I felt the ripple." She knelt, fingers brushing the ground.

Right. The black hole that wasn't a black hole. "So . . . we don't know what this is?"

Lana shook her head. "We've read everything we can find."

"Nothing more in the book?" I brushed my fingers through the air as if I'd be able to feel the disturbance.

Rowan stepped forward. "It's all connected. The relics

coming together, the Shadow Realm pressing closer to ours, dreamwalkers growing stronger—"

"Stronger?" My eyes narrowed.

He shrugged. "That's what it said. But the book hasn't given us any explanation."

I clenched my hands into fists. It's not like I had any other information to contribute. Dreamwalking was only understood by those who experienced it, and even then, we were often walking in the dark.

"Tell me what I need to do." My head was already spinning. Would James feel me there? Would the presence I'd felt be there? Something warm bloomed in my chest.

Lana pulled a notebook from her pack. The edges were bent and water-damaged. She flipped it open to a bookmarked page and crouched next to me. "This comes straight from the book." She scanned the notes. "The seal needs three components: a location where the veil is thin, bloodline access— which is you—and a seal. The relic is sealed away through . . . intention? I'm not sure if I read that correctly."

Seems simple enough, my wolf snarked.

I couldn't blame her for that one. "That all sounds lovely, but how does this work logistically?"

Lana gave me an apologetic smile. "This is a theory. You know almost as much as I do at this point." She closed the book.

"But that's how it was with everything else. We didn't understand the dagger or the Shadow Realm, we still don't understand the book or the amulet, and yet it's all worked. Kind of." Mia winced, and Connor snorted.

Rowan, who'd been quiet most of the morning, finally spoke up. "I'm not Shadow Pack, but what happens with these relics affects all of us. Is this going to have ramifications for the pack? For Kitimat or Black Lake?" His alpha energy rolled off him in waves.

Lana straightened her shoulders. "Not doing something will have ramifications. And I am the alpha of Shadow Pack. I will take the consequences on my shoulders."

Destin stood next to her, his eyes hooded.

"Okay, this isn't a pissing match," Connor muttered. "Tell her what she has to do."

Lana kept Rowan's gaze a second longer, then turned to me.

"From what I can tell, you're looking for a distortion. Once I give you the relic, I'm hoping it will be obvious what comes next."

I exhaled slowly. "So I'll take it with me? The relic stays in my dream?"

"No," Lana said. "It stays in the *location* but is accessed only *through* your dream imprint. No one else can find it unless you call it back. Or . . . "

"Or what?"

She wet her lips. "Or someone cracks your mind open."

She may as well have poured ice water down my back. I remembered the amulet. The way it pulled, made it so easy to comply with James's requests.

"Here." Mia handed me a small cloth bag. I opened it to find two small white pills. "It's one cut in half. Shouldn't keep you under for too long, but you'll be out in five."

I pinched one piece between my fingers. There was no way to rationalize this decision. It was stupid. Utter idiocy. But what were my other options? To keep getting dragged toward James every night when I slept? To spend the rest of my life knowing he could find me? Or worse, use me to find the relics? I didn't know what he planned to do with them, but seeing how he used the amulet was enough to convince me it wouldn't be pretty.

I swallowed the half pill dry and dropped to the ground, lying back.

Lana crouched beside me again. "I'll go in. Once you've passed over, I'll step into the Shadow Realm to retrieve the dagger and bring it to you."

My wolf let out what could only be called a gasp. I blinked at her. "Wait—you're going in?"

She nodded.

Uh, hell no. That was not what I'd agreed to. "James is watching the Shadow Realm. He'll know you're there—"

"I'll be exposed, but we've prepared for that."

"What do you mean, prepared?"

She started talking, but the sound garbled. The edges of my vision softened as the sedative wrapped around my limbs like slow syrup. No way that was five minutes.

Lana patted my arm and stood, nodding like we'd both just come to an agreement.

"No. Lana—" I couldn't finish the sentence. The trees above me blurred and leaned.

And I dropped.

CHAPTER

SIX

Gabriel

Her presence brushed against the realm like a feather. I felt it instantly. It was nothing like the way Lana dropped into the Shadow Realm, though Erin wasn't truly here. She'd never been here, only pressing against it like a palm against a window pane.

My wolf jumped to attention as my head snapped up. "I'm aware." I spoke out loud here sometimes. Mostly to remind myself how to do it. After a thousand years waiting in emptiness—

"Not emptiness." My brother, Ansel stood at my side.

"Not even a thousand years." Brama approached, a smirk on his lips.

I nodded at each of them. "Thank you for the reminder."

"Would you like us to accompany you?" Ansel asked, his hands on his hips.

I shook my head. "No, she isn't in our realm."

Brama ran a hand over the back of his neck. "Why do we not notice dreamwalkers as you do?"

My pulse quickened. I still had a heart, lungs, a fully functional physical body here, even though it did not act as it had in the purely physical realm. I could stretch the bounds of my form. Blend with my surroundings, manipulate air, space, and time. It was a gift and a curse. I'd forgotten what it felt like to be bound and so could no longer enjoy my freedom.

I'd forgotten so many things.

"I don't know," I answered Brama. That was the truth. What I failed to mention was that Erin was the first and only dreamwalker I'd ever been attuned to. There had been many over the years. I'd run into them accidentally, unable to feel them or communicate. It was why I'd been so bold the first time Erin appeared. While she was wearing the amulet, she didn't respond or notice me. I assumed she was the same as all the others. But when she'd appeared after returning home with Lana . . .

A tingle shot down my spine as I remembered that night. How I'd sat near her, watching as she wandered like an orphaned child. Then when I spoke, she'd spun with such force, she fell to the ground.

"I'll return soon." I set off across the realm, feeling her like a beacon. I was almost positive it wasn't nighttime in the human realm, and the idea of Erin lying down for a nap during the day troubled me. I'd watched Lana, Destin, Kael, Callista, and the others from the Shadow Realm and understood what they meant to do.

My wolf whined.

"I know," I murmured as I broke into a run. That was more

communication than I'd gotten from him in weeks. When I first woke in this realm, he was almost nonexistent, so broken from—

I gasped as my chest cinched and nearly stumbled. Slowing, I tugged at my tunic, trying to get some air.

We didn't speak of that time.

I shouldn't even think it.

My wolf lifted his head before I did, ears forward, muscles drawn tight beneath my skin.

He tensed, a growl stirring low in my chest. I didn't scent danger, but my wolf surged up, pressing against the edges of me. He was restless, scenting her before my own senses had fully adjusted.

This was how it had been. Why I didn't want my brothers to accompany me when Erin entered the realm. It was humiliating to have such little control. Perhaps my wolf was just as confused as I was by this connection with Erin. Of course I'd considered the obvious. The amulet. She'd given it her blood, if unwillingly, and wore it against her chest.

I . . . well, again. I shouldn't even think it.

I crested the rise and found her lying in the grass. Her head turned to the side, her dark waves of hair splayed around her on the soft grass appearing beneath her thin frame.

That was what she wanted even in sleep. New spring grass. The realization amused me.

Her eyes fluttered open, and I expanded through the air to see them. Brown with ribbons of honey gold.

Today she looked pale. Fearful. It was as I expected, then.

Erin drew in a breath and pushed up from the ground. She turned left and right, her pulse fluttering at her throat. I wondered if she knew I was here. Each time she came now, she was never surprised to hear my voice, but did she expect it? Did she believe that I'd always find her when she dreamed?

"Lana?" Erin whispered, pressing her palms into the grass and peering through the film. Her being looked only half formed to me when she appeared like this. Like she was a spirit or ghost.

My wolf surged forward again, pulling me back to my form. Erin drew in a breath, her hand flying to the side of her neck.

He'd done that enough times for me to believe it was on purpose. *Do you enjoy her discovery of us?* I asked in my head.

My wolf merely stood at attention, his eyes locked on hers, scouring every part of her for . . . something.

"You're here." She kept her voice low, her eyes darting from one side to the next.

I moved closer. Although I couldn't show myself to her while James could seek her out, I would never make a member of our pack suffer unnecessarily. And Erin was a member of our pack. I could sense it, though I could not yet explain it. Both she and her sister, but they didn't feel the same. Mia was weak in her link, but Erin flared nearly as brightly as Lana. How could two sisters, blood related, present so differently?

"I'm here," I answered, brushing against her form so she had proof.

A puff of air left her lips as her shoulders relaxed. Did I have that effect on her? Did she feel safe with me, even in this place that she called her nightmare?

"Have you seen Lana?" she asked, her fingers threading through the grass.

"No." She'd arrived a few minutes before, but wasn't close to this location. Then again, she wouldn't be. Which relic would she try to seal first? The dagger? The book? "You hope it's the amulet," I murmured, reading the yearning in her expression. She hated it, as did I, and yet neither of us could stop thinking about it.

"Yes. Only so it can sleep."

"And if it doesn't?"

Erin wrapped her arms around herself, and I did the same, holding her so she wouldn't feel chilled. She leaned her head against my shoulder, though I doubted she understood what or whom she was touching.

"Are you the amulet?" she whispered, her voice slow and sleepy. "Do you want to hide? Stay far away from James?"

For a moment, I thought about lying to her, telling her that was exactly what I was, but my wolf again nipped at me, jerking his head and stamping his paws. "I am not." I wasn't ready to admit who or what I was, but I did want her to understand one thing. "I was human once. Like you."

Her eyes widened. "Then you are—" She paused, her cheeks flushing pink. "A male."

"I am."

"But I can't see you? Are you spirit?" Her nose scrunched. "No, I can feel you," she muttered. "What are you, then? Can I see you?"

I smiled at her excitement. She was almost childlike in her wonder. A welcome change from her normal sarcasm and dread. "You may not."

Her brow furrowed. "Are you . . . " Again, she paused, not finishing her question. She shook her head, burrowing in closer. "You protected me from James. I don't understand why, but I don't need to ask."

I closed my eyes, my curiosity itching, but didn't speak. I'd already said too much.

"If he comes—" she shivered. "Will you help me leave? Can you do that?"

"How did you come?"

"A pill. I'm here to help Lana, but she's not here—"

A howl echoed above us, and I tensed, wrapping Erin closer and turning her to face my chest.

"What was that?" she asked, her breath against my skin. Her heart beat like a rabbit against my own.

Another howl, this one more clear, and my head felt as if it might burst. My wolf cried in my head just as Erin's wolf pressed forward, staring into my eyes. The energy within me, around me, and below me flared.

You.

The word slammed into me like a thousand arrows, liquifying everything in its path. My wolf howled again, frantic now, clawing forward until I forced myself back, scrambling to clear my thoughts.

"There's been an attack!" Lana burst through the trees. "Dark creatures! Go back, Erin. *Now!*"

CHAPTER
SEVEN

Something ice-cold ripped me free of the dream, and I slammed back into my body. My head throbbed, my stomach twisted. What. The. Hell.

"Move!" Someone shouted, but the word came at me like I was at the bottom of a swimming pool. My body shook, begging to return to that feeling. Being cocooned, wrapped in warmth. Safe. Held.

Strong arms scooped me up, carrying me as I pressed my palms to my temples and squeezed my eyes shut. My wolf ran circles in my head, pacing like I'd never seen her do before.

Can you shift? Someone growled in my head.

"Me?" My voice was hoarse as whoever carried me dropped my legs until my feet were planted on earth. I wanted to go back. That brush across my skin, the rumble of his voice. Each time I dreamed, I thought about him, but this was different.

We'd actually talked, he'd admitted he wasn't the voice of a relic, which meant . . . he'd been the one touching me. Holding me.

Why was he there? How was he there? Was he another dreamwalker like me?

"Yes. Are you okay to shift?" he said out loud. I blinked my eyes open to find Connor staring down at me. "I can carry you if you need, but—"

We can shift, my wolf growled. I nodded, wetting my dry, cracked lips. *Yes. I can shift.*

On the back roads, the trucks wouldn't have made it back to town fast enough. Plus, none of us could have handled sitting in the cab waiting to arrive. The bond was mayhem. Flashes, bits of information. My wolf fought to get out, and as soon as we stashed our clothes in our packs and shifted, images poured into my head.

I gasped at the transition in my bones, the yanking in my middle, and then at what I saw.

Dead. One body. No, two?

There's been an attack.

I'd heard Lana's words in the dream but couldn't think past the flood of emotion spiraling through me at the sound of that howl. It was Lana's, I was sure of it, but then there had been another. And that sound—

My wolf gnashed her teeth, anger and grief rolling through her in waves. *What is it?* I asked, but she'd put up a wall thicker than anything I'd experienced before. I couldn't feel her thoughts, couldn't hear her voice. I could only feel pain. An ache so hot, it ignited my bones.

We sprinted through the woods, desperate to get back to aid Evelyn and the others.

Lana. Destin growled.

I'm here.

The image she sent was shaky, but she was obviously in town.

Must be nice to use the Shadow Realm to travel, Rowan grunted, dodging a tree.

The pads of my paws scraped against stone as we launched ourselves down the riverbank and over the rushing water. Traveling in the Shadow Realm was a thousand times faster than running, even in wolf form. But none of us were willing to take that risk, considering. Especially not me. My head still felt groggy, but this was one of the few times when my fast-shifting metabolism came in handy. The pill would be out of my system in a handful of seconds.

What the hell is going on? Rowan asked.

I don't know. They're just dead. The town is in a panic. Evelyn's voice shook through the bond. *I'm waiting for Liam—*

She cut off. And just when I thought Rowan might lose his mind, Liam's voice sounded, breathless. *You're not gonna like it.*

My mind scattered to a thousand different possibilities. Drugs, active shooter—

We think . . . it isn't natural. A dark creature.

Rowan skidded into a tree and yelped. *What kind of dark creature?*

Liam didn't mince words. *Vampire.*

Are you shitting me? Connor barked. *Those exist?*

My wolf whined, her thoughts still locked down. Was the bond setting her off? We'd both avoided using that mental connection—it was too reminiscent of how things had been with Nathan Black—but it proved so damn convenient.

Rowan recovered and made up the distance in time for us to slow at the edge of the wood. We shifted back, grabbed our clothes from our packs, dressed, and ran across the street into the town square.

We're on Holly, Callista called out.

The sound hit me first as we turned onto Mallard St. Sirens blaring in short, staggered bursts, voices shouting over one another, the low wail of someone crying behind the medic's tape.

Connor ran a hand through his hair. "I should've been here." Guilt was written all over his face. Those were his guys working with the panicking townsfolk.

Evelyn came running toward us from behind the bakery—barefoot, blood smudged up one arm, her braid half unraveled. Liam followed close behind, his jaw tight.

Mia broke into a jog. "Evs! Are you okay?"

Evelyn skidded to a stop, and Mia checked her over, gripping her shoulders. "Two of them. Already dead when we got there. Nothing we could do."

Connor cursed under his breath. "How are they explaining it?"

We'd all heard what Liam said. *Vampire.* There was no way in hell the humans were going to accept that explanation. They loved horror movies or spicy romance novels about paranormal events or creatures, but accepting that they existed? It would take a lot more than two pinpricks on someone's neck to make believers of them. It usually worked in our favor.

"They think it's a sick serial killer. Injections. Overdoses." Evelyn wrung her hands.

Connor nodded. "I'm going in."

"Is it safe?" Mia snatched his arm. "We've never—I've never—"

"I hope that bastard is still here," Rowan growled. He looked like he was about to put a fist through a wall.

Evelyn shook her head. "We know nothing about this. We don't know why they targeted Kitimat, and we have no idea how to eliminate this threat."

Liam jerked his chin toward the alley behind the pharmacy.

"They were kids. Seventeen, maybe eighteen. Still had their school ID lanyards on."

My stomach lurched. Callista looked like she was about to be sick.

Rowan's face turned a dangerous shade of red. "I want to see them."

Evelyn's mouth opened and closed, then she nodded and led all of us down the street. We turned past the local credit union, and the scent hit me halfway down the alley. Sweat. Blood.

Two white sheets lay side by side behind a dumpster. The outlines of the bodies were painfully small. A pair of police officers stood nearby talking with Connor, heads bowed. They didn't look our way as we approached.

Evelyn took Rowan's hand, then crouched beside the first one and gently peeled back the sheet. A boy with blond curls, freckles across his nose, and a bruise across his cheek. His eyes were closed. Someone had tried to give him dignity.

Lana crouched beside Evelyn, already scanning him. "Where?"

"Here." Liam knelt on the other side and turned the boy's arm with gloved fingers. Two small punctures. No bigger than mosquito bites. No torn skin, no bruising, no trauma.

Lana hissed through her teeth. I swallowed hard and looked toward the second sheet. The girl beneath it was even younger. Short braids tucked behind her ears, lip gloss still visible on the curve of her mouth. She'd been wearing headphones. One still dangled from her sweatshirt pocket.

Even this wasn't enough to get my wolf to open up. What was she hiding? It had all started when we were dragged from the dream. Had she been hurt? Damaged?

"Who found them?" I asked.

"Delivery driver," Evelyn whispered. "He called it in, and I responded first."

I backed up a step and pressed a hand over my mouth. Evelyn was an EMT. Mia had given me the rundown on everything I missed while I was up north. She probably saw things like this every day when she lived in Seattle, but here? Not here.

For a long time, no one said anything. The wind moved down the alley, fluttering the corner of the girl's sheet.

Kael finally broke the silence, his voice thick. "We've lost our hold."

"No." Evelyn shook her head. "This has to be something else. A fluke. Some rogue, some—"

"There *are* no rogues in this territory," Lana cut in. "Not since the packs were unified."

Connor stalked over, jaw set, radio in one hand. "They're keeping it quiet. Telling the press it was an overdose. It's the only explanation that makes sense."

An autopsy would show no trace of drugs, I could guarantee that. Mia flinched beside me. Her wolf rose behind her eyes. Mine matched her energy, hackles up, fur bristling in the back of my skull. She still wasn't talking. It was starting to set my teeth on edge.

Can you tell me what's going on? I asked as calmly as I could. My wolf did the equivalent of turning her back so I wouldn't see her cry. I ran a mental hand down her back.

No one had to admit their thoughts out loud. We were all thinking the same thing, remembering the stories. The ones our parents used to scare us with when we didn't want to fulfill our pack responsibilities. Whole families drained overnight. Children found in the woods. Eyes white and throats black with rot.

But those were old stories. *Before.* Before the packs banded together and protected this entire region.

"The relics are destabilizing, the magic weakening. If our protections fail, creatures that were once locked out can start slipping through." Rowan's wolf pressed against the bond, unsettled.

He was right. I knew he was right.

"Then this is only the beginning," Connor said. "If the relics stay separate and exposed, we'll lose our grip entirely."

Lana swallowed hard. "And if we already have?"

No one had an answer.

"We need the Elders," Mia said. "We need to know how to find whoever did this. How to hunt them down."

Rowan nodded his approval.

We left Connor at the site and piled into the back of Liam's truck. He drove faster than he should have on the winding back roads, but none of us said a word. The less time we wasted, the better.

The Elder house sat on the far edge of the foothills, tucked beneath the arms of old-growth cedar and fir, its moss-covered roof barely visible from the road. The gravel drive was overgrown but the siding was newly painted, and the yard was clean.

A vehicle sat parked behind the house—an old station wagon with a dented front panel and a rusted wolf charm swinging from the rearview. The porch light flicked on before we even knocked.

Inside, Elder Marlowe sat straight-backed in a high wooden chair, his silver hair cascading over broad shoulders. His eyes, sharp and glacier gray, met mine first and held.

Across from him, Elder Tara perched cross-legged in an oversized armchair, a tea mug nestled between her palms. She looked like she'd been laughing before we walked in, the last traces of a grin tugging at the corner of her mouth. Lithe and spry, with deep lines around her eyes that made her seem permanently cheery.

"Well." She set her mug on the arm of the chair. "I was wondering when you'd come knocking."

"We weren't sure if you'd be here," Liam said.

Marlowe nodded. "You're not here to talk about comings and goings, are you?"

"No," Lana said. "We need to ask about a vampire."

That sobered whatever remained of Tara's amusement. Her posture straightened, shoulders drawn back like a bowstring. "Which one?"

"We don't know," Rowan said. "But two people were found dead this morning in Kitimat."

Tara and Marlowe exchanged a glance.

"Tell us what you found," Elder Tara commanded.

Evelyn gave as many details as she could. She narrated what she'd found at the crime scene and how people reacted in town.

Elder Marlowe's face grew stony as she spoke. "It could be him."

Elder Tara's lips drew into a line. "He would never take more than one."

"Then there were two of them," Marlowe asserted.

"Who is it?" Rowan growled.

Elder Tara drew a deep breath. "Malachai. He was deeply rooted in Terrace for a time. He was forced to leave, but has been seen near our boundaries over the years."

"Not for some time," Marlowe murmured. "If he's found a way through the wards . . . " The end of that sentence hung between us in the air. Marlowe continued, "He wouldn't have let the others loose unless he thought our pack protections were weak."

I glanced between Rowan and Lana. How much had they told the Elders? How much had they told the rest of the pack?

"Where can we find them?" Destin clenched and unclenched his hands, the muscles on his forearms cording.

"He has a right to be here if the magic allows it," Marlowe said with a wince.

Lana turned her eyes on me. "Then we have to find a way to disallow it."

"First, you will go into town," Elder Tara said.

I blinked. Into town? We'd just left town, it was in chaos, and we needed to—

"Have you forgotten it is Thanksgiving?" Elder Tara raised an eyebrow. "Your families mourn that you aren't with them. Your Kootenay pack leader and his mate have worked tirelessly to provide a pack dinner."

"But—" Lana started, and Elder Tara lifted a finger to silence her.

"You cannot ask our wolves, our magic, to run on nothing but fumes. If what you say is true, the pack needs to feel bonded. The town needs each other. You will go. You will eat. Do not put your lofty goals above the souls they are meant to serve."

CHAPTER

EIGHT

Erin

The front doors of the Kitimat Community Center yawned open, spilling the scent of percolating coffee, freshly baked rolls, and pumpkin pie. Our footsteps echoed on the hardwood.

Mia walked in next to me with Lana and Destin leading. The main hall had been transformed into something festive. Strands of colored paper leaves dangled from the ceiling, spinning lazily in the draft from the vents. Long folding tables were lined up in neat rows, each covered with donated tablecloths in mismatched colors—oranges and paisley next to faded floral.

At one end of the room, a makeshift stage had been set up with a microphone and two speakers. Handwritten signs, Relief Donations, Fire Recovery Fund, and Meal Sign-up were taped to poster boards propped against the wall.

Despite the decorations, the long faces of those inside the room belied the general weariness of the group. People spoke in low voices, hugging often, their smiles tired but real. This wasn't the bright, glittering cheer of a holiday get-together. This was survival. True community.

My heart squeezed, and Mia looped her arm with mine. "C'mon."

We threaded through the tables, the occasional nod or wave greeting us, until we spotted Evelyn near the back, speaking with Rowan. Even though we'd seen her earlier, I'd been so focused on the bodies on the street, I hadn't really looked at her.

Evelyn's usually sharp posture sagged, her shoulders slightly rounded under the cardigan she wore over her tank top. Her hair was pulled back in a loose braid. There were shadows under her eyes.

Mia and I walked closer, guilt creeping in as I realized just how long it had been since any of us had checked in on either of them. I'd been so consumed by my own problems that I hadn't spared more than a passing thought for what the rest of the pack was doing.

Not just doing. Fighting for. The relief tables. The recovery signs. The people in this hall weren't here for fun. They were rebuilding. Surviving after the fires, and now after an attack. Guilt and disappointment in myself circled in my midsection.

Evelyn turned at our approach, her smile lighting her face. "You're here. I thought—"

"We're here," Lana said, reaching out and pulling her into a hug. "What can we do to help?"

Mia, Lana, Destin, and I followed Evelyn toward the kitchen at the back of the community center. October. Thanksgiving Monday. Somewhere in the chaos of the last few months, time had stopped being something I measured. The days had blurred into one long stretch of exhaustion. I hadn't marked the changing leaves, the shortening days, the turn of the season.

How much had I missed?

The kitchen was a burst of warmth and motion. Steam curled from the roasting oven, the tang of sage and butter hitting me in a wave. Volunteers darted around with trays of rolls, pies cooling on every available surface. Liam was already elbow-deep in a bowl of stuffing, his hands moving automatically even as he turned to direct two teens carrying a bowl of trifle the size of a small boat.

"You can wash up over there," Evelyn told us, nodding toward the sink. "Then grab aprons. We're behind on the potatoes and need to plate the pies before the first round of guests arrives."

Mia and I didn't hesitate. A moment later, I was at a counter mashing a mound of potatoes until my arms ached. Mia joined Evelyn at the pie table, cutting and arranging slices, then adding a dollop of whipped cream to each.

I didn't realize how much I'd missed the feeling of working alongside my pack—just doing something normal. No plotting, no running, no fighting for our lives. Just making food. Feeding people.

The hall began to fill as we worked, the noise growing louder with boots stomping, laughter, and greetings called across the room. Entire families came in from the street, their cheeks pink from the crisp fall air.

We carried the first trays out together. There were platters of turkey, bowls of mashed potatoes swimming in butter, dishes of roasted root vegetables, and baskets of rolls that smelled like heaven.

At the first table, an elderly woman reached out, her hand catching mine for a moment before I could set down the gravy boat. "Bless you, dear," she said, her voice shaking just a little. "We wondered if this would be canceled."

I squeezed and nodded. "Thank Rowan and Evelyn. They made this happen."

The woman smiled with gratitude. At another table, two little boys argued over who got the best roll until Mia knelt beside them, splitting it in half and making them both giggle.

By the time the first round of plates was served, the hall was alive with the sounds of cutlery clinking against plates, the low hum of conversations, and the occasional burst of laughter. A young child in a knit hat toddled past me carrying a dinner roll in each fist like prized treasures.

I caught sight of Rowan at the far end, manning the coffee station and chatting with a group of older men in flannel jackets. I was refilling a basket of rolls when the front door opened again, letting in a gust of cold air. Out of habit, I glanced up and froze.

Our parents stepped inside. Mia shot me a look from the next table over. Mom still wore the same brown wool coat she'd had since we were teenagers, though the cuffs were more frayed now. Dad's toque was pulled low over his ears, but when his eyes found mine across the room, his expression shifted.

It hit me then, hard, how little time I'd actually spent with them since coming home. There'd been polite greetings in passing, quick exchanges about where I was going next, but no real conversations. No family dinners. No shared laughter.

Mia appeared beside me with a tray of steaming mashed potatoes. Her shoulders tightened for a moment before she set the tray down and said, "Let's go say hi." We walked together across the room.

"Hi," I managed, using Mia's script and setting a tray down on the table in front of them like that could make this easier.

"Girls," Mom breathed, and then she was on her feet, wrapping both of us into a hug. Dad's arm came around the three of us for a moment before we all sat down. Okay. I could do this. So far so good.

Evelyn approached with Rowan, stealing our trays. "You're done serving. Sit and eat with your family." I started to protest, but the look in Evelyn's eyes shut that right down.

The table filled with food—turkey and gravy, bright cranberry sauce, roasted squash—and for a few minutes, we kept it light. Mom asked about the trip back. Dad commented on how thin we'd gotten, always his go-to. Mia told a story about almost dropping a pie in the kitchen when a kid sneezed louder than Dad did. We laughed, really laughed.

And somewhere between passing the rolls and sneaking a second helping of stuffing, I realized something inside me had altered. I wasn't staring at them and thinking only about the day they'd chosen to stay in the pack when everything fell apart. I wasn't measuring the distance between us in years and resentment. I was listening. Seeing them. I hadn't known that would be possible for me. I wanted, maybe for the first time in years, to connect. To stop holding on to the blame.

Dad reached across the table, his rough palm resting over my hand for a moment. "It's good to have you both here."

Mia smiled. "It's good to be here."

I found myself nodding my agreement. The noise of the hall rolled on around us, chairs scraping, laughter spilling over from nearby tables. After we each had a piece of the best pecan pie I'd ever tasted, movement at the far end caught my eye.

Lana stood by the door, arms crossed, her gaze fixed on me. She tipped her chin toward the exit. The family reunion was over.

Time to go.

We moved fast. No time to debate or plan. I would go with Destin and Lana back to the logging road to seal the relic. Mia would go stay in town and find Connor so they could search for Malachai or whoever the hell this vampire was. We couldn't leave the pack alone in a time like this, so another group would stay here in Kitimat with Rowan. Callista and Kael had already arrived to help with the Thanksgiving dinner cleanup as we were walking out.

The rush, the desperation, it felt exactly as it had when I packed my things and ran north. But after meeting with my family, I wasn't willing to let that anxiety overtake me like I normally would. My time in the community center made it painfully obvious how quiet my wolf had been. I couldn't let that persist.

Please speak to me, I begged, tears beginning to prick my eyes. I didn't think I'd miss her bitterness and snark, but not hearing or feeling anything was far worse. I felt gutted, hollowed out.

It took a few minutes of cajoling, but she finally appeared from the recesses of my mind.

I'm troubled.

I nearly gasped with relief. Not the specific answer I'd hoped for, but it was something. *What troubles you?*

The wall between us thinned a touch, and grief, regret, and anxiety filtered through me, making my heart race. Something was very wrong, but there was nothing I could do to help unless she let me back in.

Our wolves were still a mystery to us, even though we were bonded. They experienced the world at an intensity our human minds could barely begin to comprehend. Almost always, this depth of feeling was connected with a mating bond. I'd never heard of a wolf having . . . mental health issues.

"All good?" Lana asked as we walked back to the edge of the woods.

"Yeah," I answered, shoving my hands in the pockets of my jacket. Before I could say more, Mia called my name. She rushed across the drive and wrapped her arms tightly around me.

"You sure you want to go?" My breath caught in my throat. I hated the idea of her being exposed or walking into some kind of trap, but what were the other options?

"We'll be fine," she said softly.

It was easier to believe that about Mia than it was about me.

We'd failed to seal the dagger. Lana had done what she could, removing it from its hiding place and shielding it with every protection she could, but we needed to get this done.

A bitter taste bloomed on my tongue. "Be careful."

Mia squeezed my hand once, then joined Rowan at the truck they were borrowing from Elder Marlowe. I watched her slide in beside him, her expression tight. He glanced at me through the windshield and nodded once before they rolled away down the gravel road.

Destin stood beside Lana, already keyed up, muscles twitching beneath the fabric of his shirt. We walked into the trees, and I stripped quickly, folding my clothes and throwing them in my pack. Lana waited ahead, already in wolf form, her silver coat catching the low light like a blade. Destin stood nearby, his hulking body tense, guarding us with the same intensity he always did when we shifted.

The wind curled against my bare skin, and I let go. The shift tore through me. The crack of bone, the sizzle of nerves realigning, the flash of heat. I gasped, or maybe I howled, I never could tell when the change stole my breath. Then I was fur and teeth and heightened instinct, paws planted in the mulch and heart pounding with something more than adrenaline.

We ran. Leaves burst beneath our feet. Mud kicked up behind Lana's tail as she led us through the trees. My lungs burned, but my body begged for more. This was the only kind of freedom I'd ever really known. Pure. Wild. Uncomplicated.

I hadn't been allowed to shift when I was with James. Hadn't had the energy to anyway. This still felt like I was getting away with something.

Emotions rolled over me as my mind settled in behind my wolf. And then the visions came. They started like splinters of light in the back of my mind. A scent I didn't recognize but felt like home. A voice laughing—low, male, rough with affection. The press of warm skin.

The image shifted—snow falling on a battlefield, a man

bleeding out in my arms, my voice sobbing his name, though I didn't know it. I didn't know *any* of this.

What the hell—

Not yours, my wolf whispered. *Mine.*

I skidded to a halt, claws digging into moss. Lana and Destin vanished ahead, unaware.

What did you say? I ran a paw over my muzzle, trying to clear the haze in my head. These images weren't familiar, but she'd just claimed them.

Silence stretched.

Then finally, she answered, *I have walked with others. But only one have I ever mourned.*

A mate. The truth of it reverberated in my bones.

Holy shit. She'd lived before. My wolf had lived another life —bonded with another woman. She'd had a mate and lost him—

The whine in my throat was involuntary. My middle seemed to split wide, my heart aching. I thought I knew my wolf. I thought we were one and the same. But in that moment, I realized I didn't know her at all.

I didn't know either, my wolf whispered. *I didn't know.*

Erin, what the hell? Lana appeared in the trees in front of me.

Is it possible for a wolf to live two lifetimes? I snapped through the bond

Lana's wolf stiffened. *What are you talking about?*

My wolf. She's lived before. She has memories—

Slow down. Lana trotted over, dropping her head and fitting it against mine. *Breathe.*

She gave me a moment, then asked, *How do you know these are real memories?*

Right. I was a dreamwalker. It would be easier to believe that I'd somehow picked these images and memories up from others or from some imaginative part of my brain, but I knew that wasn't true. I knew what I saw was real.

I just know it, I whispered, my head beginning to throb.

Lana nuzzled against me. *Okay. We don't have much time, but as soon as we finish this, I promise I'll help you figure this out. I'm your—*

She stopped short of saying that she was my alpha, probably because in the past when she'd tried to comfort me with that knowledge, it had only driven a wedge between us. My fault, not hers. I didn't have the capacity to deal with that at the moment, so all I said was, *Thank you.*

Lana led me through the trees. It felt like a hundred years since I'd left my apartment that morning. This day needed to end. I needed to sleep and process everything, if that was possible.

Seeing the aftermath of the pack's magic weakening had momentarily pushed all thoughts of myself from my head. I hadn't worried about James finding me or about the pull of the amulet since I'd seen the punctures on the teen's arms. I wasn't going with Lana and Destin for the same reasons I'd gone that morning.

I wanted to help. I wanted to seal the damn relic for all our sakes.

We emerged at the ripple just as the sun dropped below the treeline. I shifted back, skin prickling as the evening air met sweat. I stood slowly, trying not to let my hands shake. Lana and Destin gave me space, and I needed it. I needed time, too, but that wasn't something they could give.

My knees felt unsteady as I bent to pull my clothes from my bag. The denim clung to my damp skin, my sweater catching briefly on my elbow before I tugged it down. When I shoved my hand into the pocket of my jeans, I found the second half of the sleeping pill Mia had given me earlier. I breathed a sigh of relief. I hadn't thought to check for it before we left.

Lana gave a half smile as I turned to face them. "Ready for round two?"

I exhaled in a rush. "Definitely. Can't you tell?"

Destin, arms crossed, scanned the treeline. "I'll pull you out the second I get a hint that something's wrong."

I nodded, my throat tight. "Thank you."

I popped the pill in my mouth. It was chalky on my tongue, bitter enough to make me grimace as I swallowed it dry. I lowered myself to the cool, damp ground.

The edges of the world blurred within minutes just like the last time. Then I slipped into the dream realm like I was falling under water. My wolf was already awake, prowling the shadows with her ears pricked and tail high.

It took me a moment to get my bearings. *You're searching for him.*

She didn't answer, but the truth rippled through me anyway. Why had our last encounter triggered her remembrance? Of all the moments since I'd dreamwalked after James, why did this last encounter shake her like this?

Though . . . my wolf had never truly been present after we'd left James. She'd been silent, caged, distant. She'd buried herself deep when we found ourselves here. Was it the pill in the afternoon that had pushed her forward? Or something else entirely? What sparked her memory?

The shadows shifted ahead, and her head snapped toward them. We weren't alone.

I waited for the brush of air, the gentle squeeze around my middle, but it didn't come. He didn't step forward. Didn't speak.

My wolf whimpered, a low, aching sound that resonated deep

in my chest. She padded forward two steps before stopping, head bowed, tail low. *I'm sorry.* The words weren't really words—more of a feeling, a mournful, trembling thread of submission and grief.

Sorry for what? I asked.

She didn't answer. Her gaze stayed locked ahead of us, and the ache in my ribs tightened until I needed to press my palms to my chest.

But he didn't move. Didn't come close. If anything, his energy shifted back into the deeper shadow. I took a step toward where he'd been, but the space was already empty. My wolf's low growl of protest rolled through me, bitter and pained.

"Erin!" Lana's voice sliced through the air. She emerged from the darkened wood of the Shadow Realm, the dagger in her hands. Damn it. I'd been hoping for the amulet. Hopefully sealing up one relic would be enough to lessen the whole of their magic.

"Hurry," she urged, her eyes darting to the shadows.

I locked onto the dagger in her hands. "Will I be able to hold it? If I'm not there in that realm?"

Lana shrugged. "Only one way to find out."

She held it out, and I reached for it. The moment my fingers closed around the hilt, the ground—or whatever counted for ground here—gave way. It wasn't like falling. Falling implied direction. This was *collapse.*

The space around me cinched tight, crushing the breath from my lungs, squeezing until every bone in my body felt as though it would splinter. My ears rang with a high, needle-thin whine, and the air smelled of scorched metal and salt.

There was no light. No up or down. Only an infinite, suffocating *black.* My heartbeat thundered against my ribs, ragged and uneven, and still the pull deepened, dragging at my cells.

My skin prickled as if my molecules were being rearranged, rewritten.

I tried to breathe, but the air here wasn't air—it was heavy and thick, slipping into my throat like oil. My wolf pressed hard against me, her claws scraping across the inside of my mind in frantic search of something, *someone*, but I couldn't hold on to the thought. The black was swallowing even that.

Then the last of the ground beneath me vanished, and I was nowhere at all.

CHAPTER
TEN

GABRIEL

She disappeared—folded into blackness so sudden and absolute it was as if the realm itself had swallowed her whole.

My wolf reared back and howled. The sound tore through me, raw and primal, a sound I hadn't heard from him in an age. And in that instant, I knew.

It was her.

Not some dream-walker carrying a faint echo. Not a trick of the realm or a cruel shadow taking her shape. *Her.* My mate. The one I'd sworn to the stars I would find again, and again, and again.

Seraphina. The one I'd lost.

My chest tightened until I thought it would crack. The truth slid in like a blade under my ribs, so sharp I almost couldn't breathe.

I'd doubted before, even when I'd felt her presence before Erin had disappeared from the realm. Told myself it was impossible. That the bond had been severed at her death. That she had chosen another life and left me to rot in the ashes of the one we'd built.

But now . . . my wolf's voice was undeniable. *Mate.*

Anger surged hot and bitter, chasing the ache. She had *done* this to me. Her choices had chained me to a thousand years of exile, of bleeding for a cause that had outlived every oath we'd ever spoken. And yet . . .

I had yearned for her longer than I had hated her.

Even now, after lifetimes of clawing my way through shadow and ruin, after convincing myself she no longer existed, one glimpse of her in the dark, one brush of her presence against mine, and the part of me I'd buried clawed its way to the surface like it had never disappeared.

My wolf paced in my mind, restless, frantic. *We've found her. Don't let her go again.*

But she was already gone. And I could only stand there, every instinct screaming at me to dive into that blackness after her, knowing if I did, I might not come back.

CHAPTER
ELEVEN

Erin

Nothing.

No light. No sound. No ground. No sky.

There was no body here. No hands. No breath. But something warm pulsed near—no, within me.

The dagger.

I reached inward and clutched it. It was the only thing anchoring me to reality. Cold and heavy. I wrapped myself around the thought of it, even if my fingers were only memory.

What was this place?

My mind latched onto the memory of sensation. Wet moss beneath my back. The bitter taste of the pill on my tongue. The sound of Lana's voice just before the world went sideways.

I was still *me*. And I still had the dagger.

At this thought, the space around me flexed. As if the void

had taken a breath. Words and sound didn't come, but meaning did.

WHY ARE YOU HERE?

I didn't speak. I couldn't. But my answer unspooled from me like a ribbon.

A RELIC. *I have to seal it. It's dangerous. People are dying. My pack—*

No. That wasn't right. I didn't *know* if this would solve our problem. Maybe the others were wrong. Maybe this was all just some elaborate magical storybook dream, and I'd wake up with nothing to show for it but a handful of bruises and a new trauma to stuff in my back pocket.

So I showed the only truth I knew. James. The amulet. The dead teenagers.

It was still for a long moment.

WHAT WILL YOU OFFER?

THE MEANING ZAPPED through me like an electric shock. Offer? I had nothing to offer.

YOU WISH TO SEAL THIS RELIC. WHAT WILL YOU OFFER?

. . .

My thoughts scrambled. I didn't bring anything. I hadn't known I needed to.

THIS IS ANCIENT MAGIC. IT DOES NOT ACCEPT EMPTY HANDS.

The message existed everywhere at once and nowhere at all.

OR IS THAT WHAT YOU WILL GIVE? A FINGER? The air seemed to chuckle. *PERHAPS A TOE?*

My breath hitched, even though I wasn't breathing. Panic rose like bile.

NO? YOU SEEM RATHER ATTACHED TO THEM. A pause. Was I sensing amusement? *WHAT ELSE DO YOU HAVE?*

I thought about offering my kidney. People lived without one. I imagined lifting it from my body and placing it in the dark. A bloody mass on a velvet tray.

NO, TOO PRACTICAL. THAT WOULD NOT DO.

Terror quickly turned to frustration. Did the magic want something valuable? Painful?

. . .

SOMETHING YOU LOVE.

My heart, though it didn't seem to be beating, lurched. Something I loved.

Before I could think past Mia, the thought of losing her making me woozy, my wolf threw a picture into my consciousness.

THE GREAT HALL smelled of fresh rain, the stone walls still glistening from the morning's mist. I rounded the pillar at my mother's side and froze.

He knelt before her throne, head bowed, one knee pressed to the rush-strewn floor. Broad shoulders draped in black leather caught the light of the hearth, the silver clasp at his shoulder glinting like a captured star. His dark hair curled damply at the nape of his neck, and a sword—polished to a gleam—rested in its scabbard against his thigh.

I traced the lines of him as though they'd been carved for my eyes alone. My mouth went dry at the strength in the set of his jaw, the controlled stillness.

And then he lifted his head.

Our eyes locked, and the noise of the hall, the rustle of cloaks, and the crackle of the fire faded into nothing.

YES. THAT WILL DO.

THE DAGGER BURNED. Light burst in a sharp line around it, carving a seam into the nothing. A heavy sound echoed, like metal latching shut, and I was falling up.

My lungs seized as I slammed back into my body. I blinked,

limbs aching, nerves screaming. Lana's voice echoed far off. Someone grabbed my arm.

"Destin?" I gasped, remembering how jarring it had been to enter the real world again earlier that morning.

The pain in my head made the edges of the world flicker. And then—

He stepped forward. Boots crunching on soft earth. Before I could suck in a breath, his hand was on my throat.

James.

CHAPTER
TWELVE

Mia

We reached Terrace in just over an hour. Sixty-three kilometers. On paws.

My legs felt like soup, and my lungs had turned to paste about halfway through the run. I leaned against a cedar post, trying to pretend I wasn't seeing stars.

We'd changed behind a shuttered pizza shop. It was barely past eight, but the sky hung low and the smell threatened rain. Connor stood beside me, dripping sweat, his chest still rising like a bellows. His shirt was half-shredded from catching on bramble, and he looked like a movie extra from *Gladiator*. The bad kind. The one who didn't make it out of the arena. It was fairly hot.

I handed him a wipe so he could clean up a bit.

"You okay?" He scrubbed his face and hands.

I nodded and nearly threw up from the motion. "Never better."

His mouth tugged into a half-grin. "Next time, we take the truck."

I prayed there would be a next time.

The whole town looked like it had been leeched of color. Damp, gray light reflected off the glass storefronts. A Subway sign buzzed to our left, and a tiny vape shop still had its *open* sign flickering.

"This place made the ten most dangerous Canadian cities' list," Connor murmured as we walked.

"Mm. Thanks for telling me that. Right now, in this moment, as we're walking down the street in the dark."

Connor laughed and threw his arm around me. This was what I loved about him. Some men were only steady in the normal moments. My mate? He was made for a crisis.

We found a bar two blocks down—low red siding and blacked-out windows, music thumping through the cracked mortar. A faded neon sign above the door read *Digger's*.

"Charming," I said.

Connor didn't reply. His eyes were scanning the roofline, the corners of the parking lot. His jaw flexed once. Then again. The way it always did when his wolf was waking up beneath the surface. Mine was already pacing.

We stepped inside, and the heat hit me first. The bar reeked of spilled whiskey and unwashed bodies. An old jukebox played something too twangy to be considered music, and two bikers were arguing over a billiard game in the corner. Nobody looked up when we entered, but they'd noticed us.

Connor brushed his knuckles against my lower back, nudging me toward the bar. We claimed two seats, and the vinyl stools stuck to the backs of my thighs. I caught the bartender's eye—he was middle-aged, beard thick, eyes dull—

and ordered a Kokanee. Connor asked for a pint of whatever was on tap.

We put on masks of travelers, lovers on a road trip, backpackers. Transients who couldn't be threatening, but small talk wasn't happening. The most I got was a grunt from a woman who came up to order a drink, and Connor was striking out on his side of the bar.

All we needed was one conversation. One person who'd had a little too much to drink and might gossip about the town, mention strange occurrences or places we shouldn't go as visitors. After an hour, Connor exhaled slowly. "Guess that's that."

I looked at him. "What do you mean?"

He winked at me, then stood and wandered over to the pool table, a slight lurch in his step. He'd only had two beers, which was basically water for a shifter.

Shit. It took everything in my power to stay seated.

"Room for one more?" Connor called out, clapping one of the bikers on the shoulder.

The guy looked up, annoyed. "We've got the table, bud."

"Aw, c'mon. I'm not going to smoke ya or nothin'." Connor laughed and pulled the man closer.

"Hey, knock it off." The friend rounded the table, shoving Connor back.

Connor didn't let go, and the biker saw red. He lashed out, one clean hook to the jaw. I winced at the crack, remembering he had my healing abilities now.

The bar erupted as Connor lunged at the guy. Chairs toppled. A cue stick clattered to the floor before someone swung it like a bat. Shouts bounced off the low ceiling. The other biker targeted Connor's ribs, but Connor caught his arm mid-swing and twisted hard enough to make him yelp.

It was over in seconds—fast, mean, and messy. The bigger

of the two staggered back, lip bleeding, right as a bouncer built like a refrigerator wrapped one arm around Connor's chest and the other around the biker.

"You're done," the man growled. They were half-dragged, half-thrown into the cool night air, the door banging shut. I waited a second, then ran out after them.

Connor straightened, rolling his shoulders, scanning the street. The biker sniffed, muttering something and staggering a few paces away. Before he could light his cigarette, Connor was on him. He pulled him around the corner of the building, yanking him off balance and slamming him back against a brick wall.

"Tell me where you won't go in this town," he growled.

"What the hell, man?"

Connor ignored him. "Better yet, where won't the cops go?"

The man wheezed, eyes darting to the street. "I don't know what you're talking about."

Connor's knuckles tightened on his collar. "One street. That's all I need."

The biker kicked against the wall. "I don't—"

Connor slammed his other hand against the brick.

"The white house! End of town. Near the scrapyard. Red light."

"Red light?" Connor's eyes narrowed.

The man sneered. "Don't tell me you don't know what that means."

My jaw tightened. A brothel. Fantastic.

Connor grunted. "You go there often?"

The man shook his head, scrabbling against Connor's grip. "Hell no. None of us do. People who go there don't come back."

CHAPTER

THIRTEEN

GABRIEL

He touched her.

That was all it took.

I didn't think. Didn't pause to weigh the consequences or tally the risk. One second, Erin was on the forest floor, her eyes dazed, chest heaving, clutching at James's hands on her wrist and neck.

My wolf flew forward, and as fur exploded from my skin, I was on him. The impact cracked through the realm like thunder. We rolled, slammed into a tree, splinters exploding into the void. My jaws snapped at his throat, my front paws knocking him to the ground. But James grinned. Always grinning. It made me want to roast his heart on a spit.

"I wondered when you'd show." His magic surged. So much for secrecy.

80

I barely had time to dodge the first wave—pure, hungry shadow that tore the ground beside me into a pit of writhing nothing. I flipped backwards, landing hard. My claws extended, scrabbling for purchase as the jolt rattled through my spine.

James rose from the ground like smoke. I'd fought gods. Stood with the first shifters at the edge of bloodied borders, defending ancient rites and lands long since forgotten. I'd carved through armies and once challenged a vampire lord beneath the eclipse.

This was different. His strength pulsed unnaturally, and I knew the source of his power. The relics. The goblet.

A shard of memory sliced through me. Burnished gold, blood beading thick at its lip, a chant in the old tongue. My chest constricted.

I circled left. Fast. Swift like I had trained to be. I needed to draw him away from Erin. Not only Erin. Seraphina. She was there, our mate. No matter how much I blamed her, I would not let an alpha stake his claim.

James shifted and lunged. Our claws met mid-air. The blast rippled outward, violent and destabilizing. Trees bent. The ground fractured. Light cracked above us, revealing the stars of the real world bleeding into this realm.

I gritted my teeth, fighting for leverage.

James whispered in my ear. *She dreams of you, you know.*

I slammed my shoulder into his jaw, reveling in the crunch. *She's not yours.*

Ha! That makes two of us.

I drove my claws toward his chest and passed through, stumbling. He'd vanished. Slipped into smoke, then reappeared behind me, striking with a blade he hadn't held moments before.

I roared. Staggered. I dropped to my forearms as James

stood over me, chuckling. *You always did follow your heart. That's why she'll ruin you a second time.*

I lifted my gaze with blood in my mouth, rage in my chest. *You're wrong,* I growled. *That's why I'll—*

A wolf hurtled toward James, but he easily batted it away. Not it. *Her.* "Seraphina, stop!"

She whimpered, then pushed back up to her paws. She shouldn't be here. In the Shadow Realm, James had all the advantage over her. I could barely match him strength for strength, and I'd had over a thousand years to master technique.

I flung myself between them. *Go!* I barked, shielding her. But I knew that look in her eye. She was out for blood. *Please.* If I couldn't reason with her, I could at least beg. Wasn't that what I'd done the first time?

Before she could give a response, two figures cut through the dark, landing like twin bolts of silver flame.

Brama, massive and furious, his great blade already singing through the air. Ansel, his eyes aflame, all lithe precision and barely-contained wrath.

I didn't wait. I caught Erin's wrist and shoved her behind me, using the last of my energy to wrap her in a veil of concealment. She wouldn't vanish, but she'd blur.

James snarled. "You don't want her. She's tainted. You can feel it."

I bared my fangs.

He held up a finger and tisked. "And you were never good at sharing."

I nodded to Brama, then coiled to spring as the realm seemed to split open.

Lana appeared beside Erin in a whirl of shadow. Her eyes widened when she saw me.

Get her out, I growled.

Erin's—Seraphina's—eyes found mine one last time. Full of confusion. Pain. *I'm sorry—*

Lana ripped her backward, and James's face shifted from pleased to gleeful. *Yes. Let me watch your bed at night, young thing.*

I drove forward only to hear his cackle as he vanished for good. My wolf was crazed, nearly frothing at the mouth.

The realm quieted. The ground held still. Brama dropped his sword. Ansel staggered back, breathing hard.

I dropped to my belly as I waited for the wound in my back haunch to heal. It was then in the stillness that I heard a voice that had been silent for centuries.

Find her. Find my mate.

CHAPTER

FOURTEEN

The shift tore through muscle and bone, ripping the wolf from me in a rush of heat and splintering pain. Skin replaced fur, lungs shrank to human capacity, and cold air slammed into me like an unexpected wave. Knees buckled in the dirt. The forest tilted and swayed.

I struggled to breathe, then shook as I fumbled for my clothes. Fabric clung to damp skin as I dragged my clothes on, but the weight of the shirt felt like it might crush my ribs. The trees pressed in, trunks crowding closer, shadows sharpening at the edges. The scent of wet leaves and churned earth thickened until it coated my tongue.

Lana's voice cut through my mental haze. "Erin."

A hand reached for my arm, but it was too sudden. The contact lit every nerve like a brand. I jerked away, curling in tight, nails biting into my palms until my knuckles went numb. The thud of Destin's boots against the soil felt like shocks against my spine.

Lana's tone gentled. "Did it work?"

I nodded. "Yes. It's sealed." The words scraped up my throat. The relic no longer mattered. James had been there, his shadow blotting out everything else. "He tried to kill me."

Lana growled. "I know. And that wolf? The one fighting him. Big. Dark. I've never seen him before."

Grit shifted under my heel as I stared at the ground. A lie weighted my tongue, but the truth burned hot and unyielding —broad shoulders, a face half-lit by darkness, a gaze I knew. Gabriel.

None of us had seen him, but I'd watched him shift when he attacked James. That was who stayed in the dreams with me. I knew it with certainty, but it didn't make any sense. Why would Gabriel comfort me there? Talk with me? Protect me?

Lana crouched in front of me, eyes steady, voice low. "Erin. You have to breathe. You can't stay like this." Her words slipped through the fog in my head but didn't stick. Before I could respond, Lana shot up. "What are you—"

"I have moments only." A warrior, not Gabriel, stood in front of us looking like he was in Gladiator cosplay. "We only leave the Shadow Realm when the lives of our pack members are in danger."

Lana nodded, sending me a message through the pack bond. *I've seen him before he came with Gabriel to the rock, when I found the book.*

His eyes were as dark as volcanic glass. "She's linked to the relics. James can feel that mark as easily as you can feel the pull of your own wolf."

Lana's jaw flexed. "So you're saying—"

"He tracks her. She's tethered to their dark energy."

"Because of the amulet," I murmured. "Because of James."

The warrior's brows pulled together. "Every time she is close, she burns brighter to him."

Cold slid down my spine. "Then I'll go further away."

"That's not how bonds work. You can't run. But we believe you can hide."

We. Was this Gabriel's doing? Why hadn't he come to deliver this message? My wolf whined at that thought.

"Hide where?" Lana clenched her hands at her side.

Brama stepped closer, the weight of his presence pressing against my chest. "In the dark."

"I don't think this is what he meant," I snapped as the truck bounced along the highway.

"It's exactly what he meant." Lana pursed her lips. She didn't like it either, but that didn't mean we weren't going to do it.

My wolf prowled in the cage of my skull, claws scraping the inside of my ribs. *We should be looking for him.*

The name she didn't speak throbbed in the air between us. *Gabriel is gone,* I snapped back. *We don't even know why he was there.*

Her pacing intensified—hot breath, restless muscle, the steady thud of her paws against my mind. *Find him.*

Why? Why are you obsessed with him?

Silence. Then a flicker of images so quick they cut. Strong hands catching my waist and spinning me, the two of us laughing breathlessly in a sunlit field. The low, rumbling sound of a man's voice teasing me in a language I didn't know but somehow understood. A thumb brushing across my cheekbone, tender and certain, like it had done so a thousand times before.

My stomach clenched. *Those memories aren't mine.*

They're mine, she answered, and the weight of her meaning hit harder than claws. For a moment, I was speechless. Mine? My wolf was one with me—I was born linked to her. How could—?

You've lived before. Betrayal burned. *And you didn't tell me.*

The silence in my own head was deafening. I didn't know.

I scoffed and turned toward the window.

"Something you want to share with the class?" Lana asked, turning to peer over the seat between us.

"My wolf is a stubborn asshole," I muttered.

Lana laughed out loud. "Join the club."

Gravel hissed under Destin's tires as we left the logging road, the darkness swallowing the forest behind us. The low rumble of the engine rocked me into a half-sleep I couldn't hold on to.

Conversation in the front seat blurred into static. Lana's voice floated in and out. Every time the truck jolted over a rut, my eyes cracked open to trees ghosting by in the moonlight, then slipped shut again.

My wolf remained silent, and I was glad for a little privacy. While I was pissed that my wolf had kept this from me— because how could she not know she'd had another life—I'd committed the same crime. I didn't tell Lana the truth. I had no explanation for it, except that the idea of admitting that Gabriel was the wolf we saw made my stomach cramp. He hadn't shown himself to me or anyone else since we returned from the north. There had to be a reason for that, didn't there?

When I surfaced fully, the mountains had pulled back, and

a scattering of lights bled into the sky. *Welcome to Terrace.* The main street stretched ahead, half-asleep under flickering lamps. A 24-hour diner buzzed in the corner window, its neon sign sputtering. Two bars still had lights on. The rest were boarded storefronts, shuttered gas stations, and ghostly streetlights.

"Any word from Mia?" I asked.

Lana shook her head. I didn't know what that meant, but it couldn't be good.

Destin muttered under his breath, leaning forward over the wheel, and then the truck jolted hard. A thump under the tires, sharp enough to throw me forward against the seatbelt.

"Shit," he hissed, braking hard. The smell of hot rubber bit the air as we skidded to a stop.

When I looked up, the headlights carved a pale figure out of the dark. Tall. Gaunt. His coat hung straight to his boots.

The beam from the truck lit the planes of his face. He had sharp cheekbones, skin too pale to be natural, lips curved in a smile. And those eyes. Black, glinting red at the edges.

Destin turned off the truck and shoved his door open. The hinges groaned. "Stay in the truck," he ordered. The cold night air rushed in, sharp as knives, and I shivered.

The man didn't move. Didn't blink. His head tilted the barest fraction, like a predator testing the air. Lana slid her hand toward the door handle. My wolf bristled, muscles tightening under my skin. Every instinct screamed that something was wrong.

"Looking for someone?" The man's voice was silk over steel.

Destin didn't answer, just shifted his stance, weight settling in a way that meant he was ready to strike. The wind changed, and the man inhaled. Slowly. His smile widened, revealing the faintest glint of teeth that were too long, too sharp.

Lana's eyes narrowed. "Vampire."

The creature's eyes snapped to her through the windshield. His grin sharpened. "Good. Saves me the trouble of explaining."

CHAPTER

FIFTEEN

Destin watched the vampire like he was waiting for him to vanish into smoke. The man only turned, long coat swaying, and began walking down the road without looking back.

"Guess we're following him," Lana muttered, already unbuckling.

We fell in behind him. The streetlamps here were few and far between, their yellow glow swallowed by the surrounding dark. Each step away from Main Street made Terrace feel emptier.

I kept my gaze on the vampire's back. My wolf paced tight circles in my head, every muscle twitching, hackles up. *This is wrong. He's wrong.*

I know.

But my thoughts kept circling the real question. Was this

90

the one who drained those two teens in town? Did he have Mia and Connor, or had they never made it this far? My heart hammered in my chest.

The paved road gave way to dirt. Houses appeared here and there, all dark except for one ahead, a plain two-story farmhouse crouched at the edge of the treeline. Its siding was weathered, paint peeling in long strips. A rusted wind chime dangled from the porch, twisting without a breeze. Above the porch steps, a single red light glowed.

"Hell," Destin muttered under his breath.

The vampire stopped at the gate. Hinges screamed as he pushed it open and gestured for us to pass. The grass on either side of the walk stood too tall, whispering against our jeans as we followed the cracked concrete path. The boards of the porch groaned as we climbed the steps.

This was a shit plan. I couldn't be here, and I certainly couldn't stay here. I needed to think of a different option—a different way to hide from James.

The vampire reached the door and placed his hand against it. "Welcome," he said, voice low and oddly formal. The latch clicked, and the door swung inward.

My eyes swept the living room. The beige carpet was worn in familiar footpaths. There was a brown plaid sofa that sagged in the middle, side tables with mismatched lamps, and family photos lining the walls in wooden frames. Smiling faces at summer picnics, toddlers in Halloween costumes. It was so ordinary, it made me sweat.

The kitchen beyond was no different. Oak cabinets from the late '80s. White appliances with magnets scattered across their fronts. A calendar with kittens hung beside the fridge, a red pen circling the month's doctor's appointments and grocery runs.

The vampire crossed the linoleum and stopped at a door

tucked beside the pantry. He opened it without a word. Wooden stairs descended into a basement lit by a single bare bulb. The air down here smelled of laundry detergent and cement.

Washer. Dryer. Card table stacked with jigsaw puzzles. A shelf of neatly labeled canning jars. Completely normal. Until he pressed his palm flat against a section of wall.

A click. A hiss.

The drywall swung inward like a door, revealing darkness and the thump of bass so deep it shivered my ribcage. Light pulsed from somewhere beyond, red and gold spilling into the narrow opening.

Lana's gaze flicked to mine. Destin's mouth flattened into a line.

The vampire stepped through. We followed.

The hidden hall opened into a cavernous space that had no business existing under a farmhouse. Gold-veined marble floors reflected crimson light from chandeliers dripping with crystal. Velvet drapes in shades of black and burgundy framed alcoves where couples tangled together in shadow. The air was thick with perfume and something more primal beneath it, coppery and sweet.

My wolf recoiled, her hackles lifting, claws flexing in my head. It was like stepping into the most opulent sin I could imagine. Polished brass poles rose from platforms where dancers moved in slow, deliberate rhythm, their eyes half-lidded, skin glowing under the warm light. Low couches upholstered in black leather curved around glass tables laden with champagne, crystal decanters, and bowls of sugared fruit.

Servers in lace corsets and silk garters wove between patrons, some human, some not, balancing trays of drinks and plates of chocolate-dipped strawberries. The bass thudded through the floor, steady and sensual, matching the slow pulse of bodies swaying in time.

The scent made my head swim. Perfume and lust. Every nerve in my body hummed with wrongness.

The vampire moved through it like a king returned to his court and never once looked back. Eyes turned as we entered. Vampires lounged in shadowed alcoves, their stillness almost theatrical, but their gazes sharp and predatory. One lifted a glass filled with something far too thick to be wine, his smirk curling as his tongue swept the rim. Another leaned against a pillar, a woman pressed to his chest as his mouth moved along her throat, fangs grazing but not breaking skin. Yet.

In a corner, a pair of humans tangled together, limbs slick and glistening in the low light, their pleasure amplified by the vampire sprawled behind them, his hands and mouth everywhere at once. My wolf recoiled, the urge to snarl rising up in my own throat.

I glanced at Lana and Destin. They were stiff, eyes locked ahead, deliberately avoiding the heat-drenched displays around us. We wound through the club until we reached a set of black lacquered double doors. The vampire pushed them open, revealing a room that felt more private but no less brazen.

A man lounged on a velvet couch like it was a throne, two women draped over him, one feeding him grapes while the other traced a slow line down his chest. His eyes, dark and glinting with amusement, fixed on Erin as his mouth curved into a grin. It felt like a hook sinking in.

"Well," he drawled. "Took you long enough."

It wasn't until Erin's eyes adjusted to the dimness that she saw them. Mia and Connor sat at the far end of the couch. Mia's eyes were wide. She gave one quick shake of her head. Then the door clicked shut behind me, sealing us all inside.

CHAPTER
SIXTEEN

The veil between realms shimmered, thin enough for me to see every detail. The vampire sprawled like a king in his den of velvet and shadows, two women tangled over him as if their bodies existed only to amuse him. One fed him from a crystal bowl, the other's hand slid lower, deliberate, possessive. My wolf snarled, pacing along the edges of my control.

I didn't want Erin anywhere near this debauchery, even if it had been my idea to send them there. She needed to hide. This energy was so dark, James would never feel a hint of her presence. That didn't mean I had to like it.

The vampire's voice cut through the thrum of bass. "It's so rare we get visitors of your caliber," he purred, his fingers trailing lazily over one woman's bare thigh. "Terrace is a small town, after all. Not much to keep . . . interesting company." His gaze moved to Erin, and my chest tightened. "But tonight," the vampire went on, "tonight might be worth remembering."

Erin didn't answer. Her shoulders were tight, jaw set. She kept her eyes anywhere but on the vampire's lap.

I couldn't keep my eyes off her. I hadn't intended to look at her this way—hadn't allowed myself to even though I'd been pulled to her night after night. But here, surrounded by this deliberate, throbbing decadence, I noticed everything. The way her hair brushed her jaw when she turned her head. The way the amber flecks in her eyes caught the light. The delicate line of her throat.

Memory pulled me backward. Seraphina, lying beneath me in the candlelit chamber, the night air heavy with the scent of summer rain. Her fingertips tracing the ridges of muscle along my stomach, not to tempt me but to know me, every touch a wordless vow. Her kiss was never just hunger. It was recognition, a claiming of something that went deeper than the flesh.

The same yearning coiled low in my belly now, fierce and unwelcome. I imagined cupping Erin's face, brushing my thumb across her cheekbone, feeling her breath catch beneath my mouth. I imagined her fingers in my hair, the taste of her— new and yet so familiar it scraped against that part of me that still bled.

But reality in the Shadow Realm was cruel. My body here was a weapon, not a man's. I hadn't touched anyone—not truly—since the night I'd lost my mate. And as much as the ache in me grew, the grief was sharper. What if I couldn't do more than brush her with shadow? What if all I could ever do was watch her from behind this unbreakable wall?

My wolf pressed at the edges of my mind, not with hunger, but with an echo that tore me in two. *Mine.* His claws dug into the nothingness beneath his feet, the Shadow Realm pulling taut around us like a net.

We leave her here? My wolf snarled. *With that thing?*

You know why. James can't reach her here.

My wolf's growl deepened, vibrating through my bones. *I don't care. I will not watch her be near him.*

You think I want this? I pleaded with him. *You think I haven't suffered enough? You showed me that it's her. Our mate. I feel the same grief.*

For a moment, my wolf's pacing slowed. *Then why do you keep her at arm's length?*

My breath hitched. *Because I can't . . . not after Seraphina.* Her name was a blade, cutting open an old wound. *She had to sacrifice.*

My wolf's ears pricked. *She sacrificed you.*

Yes. The word burned. And I had chosen the Shadow Realm. To watch, to guard. I was her mate, but she traded me for them.

Silence stretched, thick with grief neither of us had dared speak of in a millennium.

My wolf's gaze softened, but the ache in my chest was a vice. I'd longed for her through centuries of emptiness, and now here she was—reborn—and I couldn't have her.

Lana's voice ripped me from my self-pity. "She needs to stay here. You're the only one who can keep her hidden from him."

The master vampire leaned back, a slow smile blooming like blood in water. "Ah. Here I thought you were displeased with my presence, but it is I who you ask for help. Humble Malachai."

Connor's jaw flexed. "Don't get used to it."

A soft laugh rolled from Malachai's chest. "As you know, everything comes at a cost." His gaze slid to Erin, lingering there, cold and hungry. "Do you know what we do here, my love?"

My mouth went dry. I didn't answer, so he went on, voice dripping with self-indulgent pleasure.

"We deal in pleasure. For us, everything is heightened. Every sound, every taste, every sensation—more vivid than you can imagine. And we can have whatever we want, whenever we want. Which . . . " His smile turned wistful, almost bored. " . . . gets tedious." He tipped his head, eyes glinting. "I have learned to savor patience. To draw out the wanting. Sometimes for hundreds of years."

Malachai lounged deeper into the velvet couch, the women on his lap shifting like cats in heat. One trailed her tongue up his throat. The other's fingers slid beneath the open collar of his shirt, nails scratching just enough to lift the skin.

He didn't look at them. His eyes, black as polished obsidian, were fixed on me. He raised a hand, and the women stilled instantly, their lips hovering just shy of his skin. "Protection is such a delicate thing," he said, stroking one woman's jaw with the backs of his fingers. "Too much of it and you forget what you are."

His gaze cut back to Lana. "We'll keep her safe. She will eat better than she's ever eaten in her life. Warm baths drawn for her every evening. Hands to ease the knots from her muscles." His eyes flickered over her like a caress. "We'll see she sleeps in silk or nothing at all, her choice. That she never lifts a finger."

Malachai's smile sharpened. "And each night I will come to her. Not to take—oh no." His voice was honey over broken glass. "Just to remind her she's mine. While she's here, of course."

A growl ripped from my throat. Every fiber of me strained to cross over and end the vampire where he sat—languid, grinning like the bastard he was.

Malachai leaned forward. "For this service, I want only a prick of blood each day. I will command my vampires that they may not touch her—only sit, and watch. They will feed her. Massage her. Dote on her and treat her like a queen." His lips curved with something that was neither smile nor snarl. "And each night, they will smell her blood knowing they will never have her." He pressed a hand to his chest, closing his eyes as though the image was too exquisite to bear.

My wolf threw itself against the inside of my skull, howling to break through. But he couldn't. I had no power here, and that realization sent me crashing to my knees.

CHAPTER
SEVENTEEN

ERIN

The vampire's words hung in the air like smoke, thick and suffocating. My wolf paced behind my ribs, claws skimming bone, snarling at the thought of being caged here, of him touching me, of his scent clinging to my skin.

Lana's voice cut through the pounding in my head. "There has to be another way." She leaned forward, elbows on her knees, her eyes locked on the vampire. "What if one of us stays instead?"

Destin's jaw was set, the muscle ticking. "I'll do it. I can keep them in line."

The vampire's smile was gentle, but the temperature in the room dropped. His hand slid from the thigh of the brunette on his right to the armrest, a lazy movement at odds with the ice in his eyes. "No."

99

One syllable, quiet, but it landed like the crack of a whip. The women on his lap stiffened, then he shoved them off without looking, their bodies hitting the rug in a tumble of silk and bare skin. "Only her." His gaze held mine, unblinking. "That is my price."

My stomach twisted as my wolf surged up, snapping to get out, but I shoved her down. If I let her take control now in this place, we wouldn't walk out alive.

Lana's lips pressed into a line. "Then we'll stay close. All of us in town. She doesn't set foot here without—"

"You can loiter in whatever holes you please," he said, his tone dripping false courtesy. "But she remains here, in my care. Or not at all."

Destin's hands curled into fists. I could almost hear his molars grinding. It was useless. I knew it, even if my wolf couldn't accept it. If I didn't stay, James would find me and probably the relics before I could seal the others.

"Fine," I said, before Lana could argue again. My voice came out steadier than I expected.

We'll be here in minutes. Just call, Connor sent through the bond.

Thank you, I sent back.

The vampire leaned back into the couch, satisfied. "Then we have an understanding."

My wolf slammed herself against me in protest, but I kept my face still. I'd made the choice. Now I'd have to survive it.

My friends left before I could second-guess my decision. The door clicked shut behind them, muffled by the thick carpet, leaving me alone with one of the vampire's silent attendants. She led me down a narrow hall, the pulse of bass vibrating the walls.

The woman opened a door near the end, and for a moment, I forgot where I was. Soft gold light spilled across the room, catching on silk drapes that hung like liquid sunlight from a canopy bed carved in dark wood. A chaise sat near the window, upholstered in cream velvet. The bath was set in an alcove, a freestanding porcelain tub surrounded by jars of oils and salts.

A low table in the corner held a tray of food: thick slices of bread still steaming, a wedge of sharp cheese, berries glistening under a drizzle of honey. A crystal decanter caught the lamplight, the amber liquid inside beckoning. Every luxury was within reach, but it all reeked of him. Of control dressed as generosity. My wolf paced in circles, refusing to lie down.

I didn't touch the food. Didn't go near the tub, no matter how much my muscles ached. I stripped down to my shirt and crawled into the bed, pulling the coverlet up without letting my skin brush the silk sheets more than necessary. Refusing to take pleasure in it. *Do you know what we do here?*

I would stay here until the amulet and the book were sealed. Until James's grip on me shattered. Then I would walk out of this house and never come back.

EIGHTEEN

Erin

We rushed through the corridor, breathless, trying to stifle our giddy laughing. The muffled clang of practice swords rang from the training arena beyond, but here at the far back of the empty barracks, it was only the two of us.

Gabriel closed the door and lowered the latch, then crossed the room to me. His hands framed my hips, pinning me against the wall. "Dangerous to find me here." His breath was hot against my throat, and every time his lips grazed my skin, my knees threatened to give.

"Will you be missed?" I teased.

He smiled against my jaw, wicked and sure. "Let them miss me."

One hand caught the hem of my skirt and pushed it upward, the calluses of his fingers grazing bare thigh. My back arched against the stone, the rough surface biting into my shoulder blades. His body pressed flush against mine, heat radiating through the thin barrier of his tunic.

My breath hitched at the clink of his belt, then left in a rush at the feel of him.

"Are you alright?" he whispered, his voice rough.

"More than alright." I curled my fingers in his hair.

He moved hard and fast, the urgency of this stolen moment making patience impossible. I pulled his mouth to mine, swallowing the groan that rumbled low in his chest. His grip on my thigh tightened, lifting me higher, and the sound of my back striking the wall in rhythm with his hips echoed in the empty room.

It ended as quickly as it began, his forehead pressing to mine, both of us trembling. He kissed me once, deep and slow, as if trying to brand it into memory before lowering my skirt. "I'm sorry I can't stay to—"

"No, go," I laughed. "Come to me tonight."

"I promise." He kissed me again, then turned toward the door.

I leaned against the wall, still catching my breath, flushed and laughing as he ran back to his drills, the sound of his boots fading into the clangs and shouts of training.

I cleaned up and ran the whole way back to the castle, boots snapping through puddles left by the morning rain, skirts clutched in my fists. The heavy wooden doors gave way under my push, the familiar scent of beeswax polish and old stone rushing over me.

The corridor was dim, torches banked low, the quiet echoing my hurried steps until voices drifted down from the sitting room ahead, my mother's among them, low and measured.

I slowed, heart thudding for an entirely different reason now, and pressed my back to the cool wall beside the archway.

"…it is unraveling," she said, her tone sharp. "The darkness is hungry. It presses closer every year."

A man's voice, older, answered her. "Shifters have always held the balance. We are the line between the mortal realm and the shadow. But your Shadow Pack." He scoffed. "They grow prideful. Less willing to serve the rest of the packlands."

"Not just unwilling," my mother murmured. "Resentful. Their magic knows it. It's twisting in answer. The more they resist their purpose, the more it resists them."

A pause. I held my breath.

"If we lose their loyalty," the man said finally, "we lose our strongest shield. And the darkness will come in full."

I pressed my palms to the stone, knuckles whitening, their words settling like cold lead in my chest, then slipped away before either of them could catch me listening.

My chambers were dark, the shutters drawn tight against the afternoon light, but I didn't bother with candles. I knew every shelf, every drawer by memory. The small cedar chest beneath my bed scraped against the stone floor as I pulled it free. Inside, the familiar scent of dried herbs and oils rose to meet me—sharp sage, sweet yarrow, the grounding musk of valerian. I set out jars and vials, the silver-etched mortar and pestle, the worn leather book whose pages were soft with years of turning.

Not the charms for warding hearths. Not the tinctures for fever or bleeding. These were older workings, pieces of knowledge I'd never dared use. Until now.

My fingers hovered over an inked diagram, a binding circle laced with runes I'd traced a hundred times in study but never attempted. The text spoke of anchors, vessels that could carry and hold great magic, tying it to the bearer's will. Objects of power.

The thought sparked like flint. If the Shadow Pack could be

bound to their purpose—no, if their selfishness and pride could itself could be kept at bay through crafted relics, they might yet stand. We could keep the darkness at bay.

I turned the idea over, breathing in the mingled perfume of rosewood oil and crushed myrrh, my mind racing ahead to the possible shapes those relics could take. Rings. Blades—

Erin.

A whisper slid through the dark. The pestle slipped in my grip, clinking against the mortar. I scanned the room, heart thudding.

Erin.

The voice curled under my skin, familiar and wrong all at once. The names in my head didn't match. *Seraphina. Erin.* Both mine and not mine.

Then the realization struck like cold water.

I was dreaming.

The darkness in the corner shifted. A figure stepped forward into the thin spill of moonlight.

Gabriel.

CHAPTER
NINETEEN

GABRIEL

Her scent hit first, and my wolf prowled forward before I could stop him. She stood a few paces away in the dream-space, all pale light and steady gaze, but the set of her jaw carried an echo of the girl I'd known in another life. I saw the dream. That memory pulsed in me, aching like an unhealed wound.

We circled each other at first without moving, letting our wolves do the work. Mine paced inside my skin, nostrils flaring, pulling in every note of her scent like it could anchor him. Hers brushed against my mind's edges, cautious, wary, but unable to mask the spark of recognition. The air between us thrummed with it.

"Where are we?" she asked, voice low, as if afraid too loud a sound would shatter the strange tether holding us here. "Am I in the Shadow Realm . . . or are you here with me?"

She was nervous and had every right to be. "I'm not sure." I let my gaze track over her, memorizing every detail. The stubborn tilt of her chin, the way moonlight caught in the strands of her hair. "Wherever it is, I've been waiting a long time to stand here in front of you again."

Her eyes searched mine. "Did you see it? The dream?"

"Yes." The word scraped my throat raw. The memory hit with a force that stole my breath—her laugh in the corridor, her sigh against the barracks wall, her hands gripping my shoulders, the heat of her skin under my palms.

That day in the practice yard had been reckless, impossible, perfect. We'd claimed each other as mates the night before, alone beneath the old stone arches while the world slept. We'd known what it meant—how the law would see it. She was Shadow Pack, bound by oath to choose one of her own.

I was not.

We'd agreed to wait. To keep our bond hidden until we could find a way to make it possible. And then, in the barest sliver of time we could steal, she'd pulled me out of the practice yard. Breathless. Laughing. Mine.

Grief and pleasure tangled in my chest until I couldn't tell one from the other. I'd lived a thousand years on the edge of that moment, the echo of her laugh my only companion in the dark. And now she stood before me again. Different and yet exactly the same.

"Why didn't you show yourself?" The question was sharp, and it wasn't only her voice.

Her wolf prowled under her skin, eyes brighter, gaze more direct as if she'd shoved Erin aside to demand answers.

The truth tasted bitter. "Because James is becoming more

adept in the Shadow Realm." I stepped closer, letting her see the weight in my expression. "He's tainting it, pulling on anything with power, even the protections of the Shadow Pack. I thought if he knew I was here, if he knew Brama and Ansel existed—"

"Those are the others?"

I nodded. "I thought he'd tear this place apart to get to us. I couldn't risk it."

Her wolf stilled, measuring me. But Erin . . . Erin's gaze flickered between my eyes like she was trying to decipher me.

Every movement she made pulled at the tether between us, the one I'd spent a thousand years trying and failing to sever. Want surged in my blood, raw and dangerous. My wolf strained toward her, but I locked my jaw against it. Need warred with the memory of what she'd done—what she'd left me to become.

"You left me there." My voice cracked low, the words laced with a thousand winters' worth of rage. "You—Seraphina— forced me to live without a mate. Because of the relics."

Confusion tightened her brow. "I—" She paused. "I don't know the whole story."

I almost laughed. "She hasn't told you?" Had Seraphina's wolf lived in Erin's head without giving her a hint of the truth? "It's not my story to tell."

For a moment, the dream-space thickened, the air between us charged with too many truths left unsaid. My hands itched to touch her. My mouth ached to taste her again. And yet the wound she'd left in me was still bleeding, all these centuries later.

Erin's wolf stepped back, letting her regain control. She lifted her chin, breath steadying. "We need to talk about the relics. If I can seal them all, I can get the hell out of that lair before James even realizes where I am."

My focus narrowed on her, on the flush in her cheeks that deepened when she glanced at me, only to dart her gaze away. She waited for my reply, her eyes slipping to my mouth before she caught herself. My wolf rumbled low in approval.

"You can seal them," I said slowly, "but James will still be searching for the source of the disruption in their power. He's tied to them. He'll feel it."

She began to pace. "Then we make sure he's looking in the wrong place."

"What are you suggesting?"

"A distraction. What can you offer?"

I wet my lips. "Does this conversation come at a cost?"

Her eyes flared. "That's all I'm ever told."

I considered this, thinking a moment before I told her how I could move in the Shadow Realm, how I could manipulate the darkness around Lana—make it look like she was the one carrying the relic. "He'll chase the false trail, and you'll finish sealing the relic without him breathing down your neck."

She looked up, and her mouth quirked. *When had she gotten so close?* "You'd risk that?"

"I'd risk more than that." The words slipped out before I could stop them.

She didn't flinch. Erin was only a foot in front of me, and the scent of her was sharp and heady, the heat from her skin brushing mine.

"Gabriel . . . " Her voice was a whisper, but it carried in this place. Every instinct in me screamed to take her mouth with mine, to feel the truth of her pressed against me. But my anger still coiled in my chest, dark and poisonous, and if I touched her now, I wasn't sure whether it would be out of love or punishment.

We stood there, caught between the weight of our plan and the gravity of the pull between us. Neither of us moved.

Ten seconds. Maybe less. My understanding of time was permanently altered.

I remembered the rush of her breath when we'd claimed each other as mates under the cover of night, knowing it was forbidden, knowing we'd never be allowed. I'd told myself back then that no force in this world or any other could keep me from her. And yet, here we stood, proof that I'd been wrong. About everything.

Her voice cut into the space between us, soft and steady. "What has it been like for you?"

The question hung in the space between us. Did she wish to unburden herself from the guilt of her sacrifice? Images flashed unbidden—endless darkness broken only by silver light, the weight of silence pressing against my skull, the cold ache of centuries without her. And the fighting. Clawing to protect what scraps of our pack still remained.

Her gaze searched mine. "You can touch here," she said quietly. "You can feel."

I cleared my throat. "Yes." But I hadn't touched her or anyone else with flesh and blood.

Then she extended her hand between us, palm up, like an offering. Every instinct screamed at me to step back, to keep the boundary intact, to protect what was left of myself. But I didn't.

I reached out, slow enough to be aware of every shift of muscle in my arm, and pressed my fingertips to hers. The contact was electric. Heat bled into me from her skin, chasing the cold from my bones. My wolf pressed hard against my ribs, hungry for more.

I'd gone without her touch for a millennium. And in that moment, it was like drinking after years in the desert. Her lips parted. My pulse thundered. The distance between our hands narrowed, our fingers curling together before either of us thought to stop it.

I didn't know if I wanted to pull her into me or drop her hand and run, but I chose wrong. Or maybe I chose exactly what I had to.

My hand lifted before my mind could protest, fingers trembling as they found her cheek. The same way I had a thousand years ago, when I didn't understand why I couldn't stop protecting her. Why she pulled me like gravity, bending every oath I'd made to the pack.

Her skin was warm under my palm. Guilt knotted low in my chest, twisting with a sense of betrayal—not hers, but mine. I wasn't supposed to touch her. I couldn't do anything here. Not with the new oaths I'd made. This time I didn't have control over that.

And yet I had to.

My thumb brushed the edge of her jaw, then drifted down the column of her throat, feeling the flutter of her pulse against my skin. My wolf surged forward, pushing against my ribs until my breath came ragged, begging for more. Begging to be with *our mate*.

I leaned in. Just enough to let my lips ghost over her closed eyelids, once, then again. She shivered. My heart stuttered. The scent of her filled me—wolf, woman, and something older that used to be mine.

I lowered my mouth, close enough that I could feel the warmth of her breath. Another inch and I'd have her. I could almost taste her, the memory of her lips from lifetimes ago flooding back so vividly that my knees nearly buckled.

Then she pulled away.

It was subtle, just a small shift, but it cut sharper than any blade. Her eyes lifted to mine, shimmering, not with longing, but with something brittle and aching.

"You want her," she whispered and took a large step back. "I'm not her." Her gaze broke from mine, and in the heartbeat before she vanished from the dream, pain settled into her features. "Watch for Lana," she said.

And then she was gone.

CHAPTER

TWENTY

ERIN

The headache hit before I even opened my eyes, sharp and pounding, like something had lodged itself behind my temples and was trying to claw its way out. I rolled onto my back, pressing the heel of my hand to my brow, but the pressure only made it worse.

The dream clung to me like smoke. Gabriel's fingers against my cheek. The heat of his breath as if he'd been about to kiss me. That almost-crushing sense of being wanted . . . and then the splintering pain when I realized it wasn't me he wanted at all. My stomach twisted, nausea curling through me.

The door opened without a knock.

Malachai stepped in, all in black except for the gleam of a ruby ring that caught the dim light. His eyes swept the room, then me, as if assessing an object he'd recently purchased.

"Up." His voice was smooth enough to make my skin crawl. "Dress. Your first day begins now."

I pushed myself upright, the headache pulsing behind my eyes, and found the clothes laid out at the foot of the bed. It was all soft fabric, rich in color, chosen to flatter, not for comfort. I didn't ask where they'd come from. I didn't want to know.

Malachai had the decency to leave while I dressed. When I stepped out, his hand closed possessively around my elbow. He didn't drag me, but there was no mistaking who set the pace.

The club was still alive even in the morning, though here, morning meant nothing. The heavy bass of the music throbbed through the floorboards, the air thick with incense and perfume, tinged with the metallic sweetness of blood. Shadows moved in the dim light, the vampires draped across plush chairs, humans entwined in their laps, glassy-eyed and pliant. It wasn't a party. It was worship.

We stopped at the center of the main floor. Conversations stilled, heads turned.

Malachai's voice carried easily over the music. "This one," he said, presenting me as if unveiling a painting. "She is under my protection. She will not be harmed." His gaze slid slowly over the room, making sure each of them understood. Then his smile curved—lazy, dangerous. "You may serve her."

Murmurs rippled outward. I couldn't tell if it was interest or hunger, but every set of eyes stayed fixed on me. My wolf pressed low, uneasy, watching every move.

Mia? Connor? The pack bond opened with a snap, raw and electric.

Erin! Mia's voice flooded in first, sharp with relief. *Are you okay?*

I think so. My eyes flicked around the club, at the vampires watching me from velvet shadows. *I'm fine for now. Malachai's making his arrangements.*

Connor cut in, his voice tight. *Arrangements? What kind of arrangements?*

Ones I'll explain later. My gaze snagged on the waiter gliding toward me—a vampire with flawless skin, his dark hair tied back neatly, holding a silver tray like it was a crown jewel. *Don't come here. Don't even think about it.*

Mia's protest hit like a whipcrack. *We're not leaving you there—*

You have to. I kept my eyes forward as the vampire set the tray at the dining table, revealing a breakfast so decadent it was absurd. Flaky pastries glazed with honey, berries glistening like spilled gems, cuts of delicate meat.

Erin— Connor started, but I shut the bond halfway, letting their voices fade into static.

"Eat," Malachai commanded.

I nodded and strode to the table. The waiter pulled out a chair, and I sat. He spread a napkin over my lap. My stomach growled, and my mouth began to water. When was the last time I ate?

I picked up my fork and tried a berry. I would have to eat, but I didn't have to enjoy it. And, if I were dining alone, I might as well use that time to remind my wolf that she had a story to tell me. *What was Gabrielle talking about? Can you tell me now?*

Silence.

I stabbed another berry, the juice bleeding into the cream on my plate. *You owe me the truth.*

A faint rustle, like paws shifting on stone, brushed the back of my mind. Then nothing. My teeth ground together. I took another bite.

When I'd eaten all I could, a female vampire approached. Her hair was black as ink and her nails like lacquered talons.

"Come. The master has ordered a massage for you. To help you relax."

The vampire led me down a narrow hall, past gilt-framed mirrors and velvet drapes heavy enough to muffle sound. The massage room was dim, lit only by a pair of low lamps that pooled golden light over a padded table.

"Disrobe," the vampire murmured. Okay, looked like she would be my masseuse. Not creepy at all.

She turned away as I pulled my shirt over my head, shoving down the instinct to cover my bare skin, then lay on my stomach. The table's leather was warm under me. Then cool hands slid over my shoulders.

Every muscle locked.

Relax, my wolf said.

You first, I shot back, my tone as sharp as the fingernails now pressing into the knots along my spine. *You don't have to be ashamed. Tell me what you're hiding.*

Silence again. Just the glide of hands down my arms, the knead into my lower back that nearly made me melt despite myself.

I'm not playing this game, I said. *You know what I saw in the dream and what Gabriel said. Why did you give him up?*

A pause. Then, like water breaking through a dam, I wasn't in the massage room anymore.

Seraphina's hands—my hands—ran over the cracked leather of an ancient tome. A book so heavy it seemed to resist being lifted, as if it knew its own importance. I—she—had taken it from the private archives of a highborn shifter family who had sworn never to part with it.

The scene shifted. Moonlight glinted off the dagger's silver edge. The weight of it in my palm felt wrong, heavy. That one had been stolen from the vault of a southern court, after a duel that ended with a man bleeding into the sand.

Then there was Gabriel. Standing before Seraphina, eyes fierce and steady as he pressed the amulet into her hand. His gift to her.

The goblet had come from a ruined chapel in the north, dug from beneath the altar, still crusted with dried blood from a forgotten sacrifice.

The crown from her mother.

It cost her, my wolf whispered finally. *More than she told anyone. Magic always costs.*

And I saw it. The night she used her runes on the book. The library warped around her, shelves twisting into shapes that shouldn't exist, the air fracturing into impossible angles. The sound of splintering wood and tearing reality. The stink of burning parchment.

That was the cost, and still she kept going.

The vampire's hands smoothed down my back, pulling me back to the present. My own breath came ragged, my jaw tight.

Why show me this now? I demanded.

Because you have to understand before—

The vampire's touch slowed, fingers pressing into the small of my back one last time before trailing away. "It is finished," she murmured, her tone the same as if she'd been reciting a prayer.

I pushed myself up, the table creaking softly beneath me. My skin prickled in the cool air as I reached for my clothes. The memories churned in my head as I followed my masseuse back into the hall.

She led me back the way we came, then turned down a new hall and stopped in front of a set of carved double doors. One stood slightly ajar, a sliver of amber light spilling across the floor.

"He is waiting." She held out a hand, motioning for me to enter. But then through that narrow gap, I caught him.

Malachai. Standing near a low table, head bent as if considering something in the palm of his hand. His silk robe hung open just enough for the light to catch on the curve of his thigh.

Metal winked there. Ornate, intricate, unmistakable.

Gold.

Gems.

My breath caught.

A crown.

My wolf hissed. Not just *a* crown, *the* crown. The same gold I'd seen in Seraphina's hands. My wolf lunged forward in my mind, teeth bared, a snarl building so fast it stole my breath.

Information clicked into place. The glassy eyes. The easy worship. He was manipulating them. All of them.

My heart kicked up. Was he manipulating us? Me? Had I unknowingly landed right back where I'd started?

Malachai flicked the robe closed with a single, elegant movement. My pulse roared in my ears. Every muscle locked. That piece of him wasn't his at all.

It was ours.

"Are you waiting for an invitation?" Malachai's voice drifted into the hall. "Because I've already given one."

He didn't rise when I stepped into his chambers. He was draped along a wide chaise, silk robe spilling over one shoulder, pale chest catching the flicker of candlelight. "You've settled in." The curl of his mouth made it sound like a verdict, not an observation. "I can smell it on you. My walls have begun to change your scent."

I kept my mouth shut, fingers curling against my thigh.

"Shifters like to think you live above us," he continued. "That you stand in the sun because you've earned it. But the only difference between us is that I've stopped lying about what I am."

He's trying to unnerve you.

"I drink from the vein, yes. I take what I desire when I desire it. But your kind?" His eyes cut to mine, the gold in them catching like a blade in firelight. "You feed just the same. Only your meat still breathes. Only your prey walks beside you, convinced they are being protected."

My jaw ached from clenching.

"That's the nobility you're so proud of," Malachai leaned forward so the candlelight carved hollows into his cheeks. "A predator in armor, pretending your power is mercy."

Don't rise to this.

"Here," he went on, spreading his hands to take in the chamber, the silks, the low-burning lamps, "we strip away the pretense. The body wants, the body takes. And in taking, we give. That is the truth your people hide from themselves. Desire is the only honest currency in this world."

I forced my eyes to stay lifted. I couldn't glance down, couldn't wait for a glimpse of the crown he wore. We had to wait.

Malachai's smile deepened, as if he'd read my want. "I have built a place where nothing is denied—except what I choose to withhold. And the absence, little wolf, is often the greater pleasure."

My stomach tightened.

"Tonight," he said, lounging back again, "you will be polished until you gleam. They will see you, but not touch you. They will ache for what is forbidden. And you, you will learn what it means to be wanted without end."

CHAPTER
TWENTY-ONE

The adjoining room smelled of jasmine. Two women waited, both human. Their eyes didn't have the glassy glaze of thralls, but I couldn't tell if that meant Malachai wasn't manipulating them or if he was simply too good at it.

They ushered me toward a sunken marble tub, steam curling from its surface. The water shimmered with gold flecks, catching the light like scattered coins. I slid in, the heat kissing every inch of skin until the tension in my shoulders loosened against my permission.

One woman knelt behind me, combing something silky through my hair. The other worked a sponge in slow, deliberate circles over my arms, my legs, her touch both clinical and oddly reverent. The water smelled of crushed petals and honey.

They drew me out, cocooning me with warm towels. One filed and buffed my nails to a glassy sheen, the other rubbed my skin with oil that smelled of citrus. They painted my lips with a sheer wine-red gloss, a little on the nose, and brushed smoky shadow over my eyes until the green gleamed like polished jade.

The woman working my hair moved with patient precision, winding the dark waves into a glossy cascade to my shoulders. Each lock caught the light like it had been spun from silk.

I barely recognized myself.

Then came the dress.

One of them unfurled it from a hanger with pride. It was black, satiny, and so short it felt more like lingerie than clothing. Thin straps left my shoulders bare, the neckline dipping low enough to make my wolf stir in irritation.

They slid it over me, the fabric cool against freshly oiled skin, and stepped back with matching smiles of satisfaction.

I stood before the mirror, studying the stranger in the glass. Her mouth was lush and dangerous, her hair liquid fire, her eyes rimmed dark like she'd just been kissed breathless. Malachai had chosen every detail.

The doors swung open on a swell of sound and the devil himself entered.

Malachai was a vision in black silk. His eyes flared. "Ah, yes. Exactly as I pictured it." He floated over to me, linking my arm with his. "Follow me, love."

I worked to keep my hands from shaking as we made our way to the club. I stepped through the door, the thin straps of Malachai's chosen dress biting into my shoulders, the slit flashing bare thigh with each step.

The music lowered. Dozens of eyes turned toward me.

It was like walking naked into my school gymnasium.

Steady, my wolf murmured, though her pacing continued. *Don't give them fear. They'll feed on it.*

They were beautiful, every one of them. Their skin glowed like marble polished by centuries, their movements slow and deliberate, as if time bent around them. And beneath it all, the hunger. It was in the way their nostrils flared as I passed. The way pupils widened and fingers clenched on upholstery, on each other's thighs, on the arms of their chairs.

"Let them see you," he whispered, moving me to stand before them. He circled me slowly, a hand trailing over my shoulder, down the curve of my back. It was possessive, deliberate—staking a claim. "You see her," he murmured to the room. "She is mine."

A ripple of something passed through the gathered vampires. Not disappointment. Anticipation.

"Look at the flush of her cheeks, the swell of her breasts," Malachai went on. My blush rose higher. Likely what he intended. "Do you want her as I do?"

A low murmur passed through the group.

Malachai looked pleased. "As I said, you may not touch."

A low hiss shivered through the crowd. The tension wound tighter, their hunger stoked by denial.

Malachai stepped in front of me again, eyes gleaming gold. "But you may watch." His hand caught my wrist, lifting it with deceptive gentleness. I tried not to flinch as he drew me closer. "This is all you may have."

From the pocket of his robe, he produced a slender silver spike, no longer than a sewing needle. My pulse roared in my ears.

He didn't ask. He didn't need to. His free hand cradled mine, his thumb brushing my palm once, almost tender, before the point kissed the pad of my finger.

Pain, sharp and bright, flared for an instant. Then the bead of blood swelled, dark and perfect in the light. Every vampire in the room leaned forward.

The scent hit them like lightning. Mouths fell open. Tongues slid over fangs. One man gripped the arm of his chair so hard the wood splintered. A woman's nails gouged deep into the thigh of the vampire beneath her, making him growl low in his throat.

Malachai tilted my hand, and the drop of blood fell—not into a waiting mouth, but to the black marble at our feet. The room shuddered. Tension crackled in the air, vibrating between the walls. Every inhale was ragged, every eye locked on the place where the blood had struck.

Another prick, another bead. He let that one slide along the silver tip, then flicked it away. Both drops wasted, each one dragging the hunger in the room to a higher pitch.

They didn't speak. They didn't need to. The sound of their breathing, the faint scrape of a fang against lip, the almost imperceptible shift of bodies as they leaned forward. It was a chorus of craving.

I could feel it, the way they imagined it on their tongues, the way their throats would work to swallow it, the burst of warmth and power they would taste. They wanted to drink me dry, and the knowledge crawled over my skin like a hundred bees.

Malachai released my wrist at last, but not before brushing his lips over the wound. His tongue caught the last trace of blood, and the groan he gave, soft, almost reverent, was worse than if he'd bitten.

The room exhaled in unison.

"You will smell her blood every night." Malachai's gaze swept the crowd like a whip. "You will watch it spill, and you will not drink. Not until I decide."

I stiffened. That wasn't our deal.

A woman whimpered. Someone's fist struck the arm of a chair. The hunger in the room was a living thing now, prowling around us.

Nausea roiled in my gut as I took in the other humans in the room. The ones who hadn't been offered protection.

"You will serve her," Malachai went on. "You will bathe her, feed her, knead the weariness from her muscles. You will keep her as I say—and in doing so, you will suffer." He smiled then, and it was terrible in its beauty. "And in your suffering, you will remember that longing is the sharpest pleasure of all."

The vampires bowed their heads, a movement so synchronized it made my stomach twist. Malachai turned me away from them, his hand warm on the small of my back, guiding me toward the stairs. The moment my back was to them, the sound of their breathing thickened again. There was a gasp. Then another. Tears pricked my eyes.

He wants them to see prey, my wolf murmured. *Let them look. They don't know you're hunting too.*

CHAPTER

TWENTY-TWO

The Shadow Realm hummed around me, the black mist of it shifting in lazy coils. I paced its borders, eyes fixed on the dim silver outline of Erin's room. My wolf was restless, its hackles raised, every instinct taut as a bowstring.

Movement.

A vampire, pale as moonlit bone, slipped down the hall toward her door. His steps were soundless, the sway of his shoulders too casual for a servant on an errand. He looked intoxicated, feral.

Then his hand rose, slow, deliberate fingers curling around the knob.

That was enough.

The tether between me and the real world yanked taut, heat roaring through me as my oath to protect the Shadow

Pack flared to life. I burst through the veil, the air around me cracking with shadow-fire.

He didn't have time to turn. My blade tore through him, the steel singing as it split bone. His body disintegrated before he could cry out, ash collapsing into a faint, gray smear on the carpet.

I should kill them all. Rip through this damned place room by room.

Go to her, my wolf growled. *This is your only chance.*

But the way they looked at her—

Go to her.

The heat of battle cooled. My pulse slowed. I reached for the door, the brass still cool from the vampire's hand. It clicked open under my palm.

The scent of the oils they'd used on her infused my senses. I hated it. It wasn't her.

She was already sitting up, hands clenching the blanket, hair mussed around her face. Fear sharpened her features until she recognized me.

Her breath caught. "Gabriel?"

I stepped inside, closing the door behind me with a quiet click. The air in here was warmer than in the hall. My wolf reacted instantly to her proximity, prowling close to the surface, familiar with her in a way my mind still fought.

She swallowed. "I heard something. Outside."

"It's gone." My voice was steady, but there was a growl under it I didn't bother to hide.

Her eyes searched mine like she was trying to reconcile what she was seeing. "How are you even here?"

"I can only cross when a Shadow Pack wolf is in danger." I held her gaze. "You were."

Her lips parted slightly, but she didn't speak. I moved to the bed and sat at the edge, keeping distance but close enough to feel the heat radiating off her. My wolf pressed harder, wanting to close the space entirely, wanting what it had once claimed.

She drew her knees up to her chest.

"You're safe here," I insisted. "James can't see you. Not in this place. He can track your energy when you're in the Shadow Realm, but here?" I shook my head. "You're hidden."

Her shoulders loosened, but wariness still shadowed her expression, and now I understood why. I'd seen it in her eyes the night she left me in the dream. She didn't trust my reasons for wanting her close. Maybe she was right not to.

I didn't know her. Not really. I knew her wolf. I knew the way her presence ignited something buried so deep inside me I'd thought it long dead. But Erin herself? She was a stranger wearing a familiar soul.

The quiet between us deepened, and I felt her wolf pressing faintly against mine, testing me, reminding me of what was lost.

Then she spoke, voice low. "I found the crown."

My body went rigid. "Where?" How had I not noticed this?

Her fingers curled into the blanket. "Malachai has it. Strapped to his thigh under his robe. I saw it when the fabric shifted."

Heat surged in my blood—rage, instinct, the primal need to reclaim what should never have been in his hands. My wolf's snarl echoed in my skull, urging me to tear it from him by any means necessary.

Erin's gaze didn't waver. "I have to get it." The quiet conviction in her voice hit harder than any shout could. "This is my chance to make things right," she continued, leaning forward, arms locked around her knees. "If I take the crown, all that's left is the goblet. Once we have that from James—"

Something in me tightened. "How will you take it?" My tone was sharper than I intended.

Her jaw set. "We'll figure it out."

That word—*we*—should have settled something in me. Instead, it twisted like a blade, pulling me back a thousand years.

Seraphina's face flickered into my mind, soft in the torchlight of the ruined library, hair spilling loose from its braid, eyes bright with that same unshakable certainty. The air still reeked of charred parchment and splintered wood. I'd told her it was enough. That no relic, no power, was worth the destruction the magic demanded.

She cupped my cheek, soot smudging her fingers. *Five,* she'd said. Always five. Each with a different power, united to push back the darkness once and for all. Her belief had been a living thing, a fire that consumed her doubts before they could take root.

I'd trusted her. And it had cost me everything.

The echo of that loss rippled through me now as I looked at Erin. The tilt of her head was different, the lines of her face not the same, but that same wild conviction burned in her eyes, and my wolf recognized it like a scar remembers the blade.

"You think this ends with a crown and a goblet," I said quietly, "but that's what she thought too."

Erin's brows drew together, confusion flickering across her face. "She?"

I didn't answer. Couldn't. Not without tearing open wounds I wasn't ready to show her. Instead, I sat back, letting the silence answer for me.

Her eyes narrowed. "So that's it? You're just going to sit here and tell me it's impossible because it didn't work a thousand years ago?"

"That's not what I said."

"It's what you mean," she shot back. Her arms dropped from around her knees, shoulders straightening, her wolf bristling beneath her skin. "You're letting your grief dictate this. You think because she—because Seraphina—failed, I will too."

The name landed like a blow. She didn't know the half of what it meant.

I forced my voice steady. "I think because I watched her bleed herself dry for those relics, and I watched the darkness grow anyway, that charging into the same trap isn't the answer."

Her gaze locked with mine, defiant. "Maybe it's not the same trap."

She believed that utterly. Just like Seraphina had, standing in the wreckage of the library with smoke curling past her hair. And that was when it hit me. Erin didn't know. Not all of it. Not the price Seraphina had paid. Not what I had lost the moment she made that final choice.

The grief rose sharp and sudden, choking me before I could push it down. My wolf shifted restlessly, wanting to stay, to protect, but the man in me knew I couldn't bear her questions. Not now. Not with her looking at me like that, like I was just another obstacle to overcome.

I stood, stepping back from the bed. Her brow furrowed, lips parting as if to call me back, but I didn't give her the chance. The Shadow Realm pulled at me like a tide, cold and relentless, and I let it take me. The room, the scent of her, the flicker of that stubborn fire in her eyes, all of it dissolved into the gray hum of my prison.

And I was alone again.

CHAPTER

TWENTY-THREE

Erin

You pushed too hard, my wolf muttered.

I swung my legs off the bed, pacing, nails digging into my palms. *You knew he'd leave?*

Silence.

What aren't you telling me? My pulse thundered in my ears. Because I watched her bleed herself dry. He'd alluded to a choice Seraphina made, and it was obvious by the hurt in his eyes that she had sacrificed him.

No, my wolf snapped. *I never would have done that.*

Her presence bristled, pacing the way she had in my head for days, but she wouldn't meet me.

Enough games, I snapped, shoving at the barrier between us. *If I'm going to survive this, I need the truth. You owe me that much.*

Her growl rippled through me, low and warning. *Some truths are teeth, Erin. Once they bite, you can't unfeel them.*

I stopped pacing, my breath harsh. *You think I haven't been bitten already?* I pressed my hands to my temples, every muscle wound tight. *Tell me. Tell me what you kept from me.*

Erin? Mia's voice cut through. *Where the hell are you? We've been going crazy.*

Alive, I responded, feeling the entire Shadow Pack tuning in. *I found the crown. Malachai has it—keeps it strapped to his thigh under his robe.*

A collective spike of tension rippled through the bond. Lana's energy bristled, a sharp current across my skin. *You're sure?*

I saw it. Up close.

Connor's voice snapped in, all steel edges. *Then we move. Now. I don't care how pretty his robe is, we go in, cut it off, and take it.*

Slow down. Destin's tone was measured but strained. *This isn't going to be as simple as slicing him open and running.*

The crown's not locked away in some vault, I said. *He wears it like a trophy. And he's using it.*

Callista's voice came in low, careful. *How? The relics shouldn't respond to anyone but—* She stopped herself, her thoughts flickering like a candle in a draft. *You think anyone can wield them?*

That's what I'm trying to figure out, I admitted. *My wolf knows more than she's saying. She's been stonewalling me since I got here.*

What do you mean by stonewalling? Lana demanded.

I mean, she's keeping things from me. My hands curled into fists in the sheets, the truth of what I'd seen knocking the breath from me. My wolf was with Seraphina. She saw the creation of the relics. She should know how they worked—

Even witches don't understand fully the magic they wield, my wolf breathed.

Connor's mental presence burned hotter. *You need to force her to talk.*

Because that works. Callista countered. *If Erin pushes too hard, she could fracture the connection. She needs her wolf to work with her, especially in a place like that.*

I bit back the urge to tell them both to shut up. *I have to stay here until we seal the next relic. I'll keep working on a plan.*

Connor scoffed. *Or we kill him faster.*

No. Destin's tone was absolute. *If Malachai dies while Erin's in that den, the entire coven will turn on her. We wouldn't get her out alive.*

Mia's voice came softer, but no less fierce. *So we work around him. Erin, where is the crown when you see it? Always on him?*

From what I can tell, yes. I paused, thinking back to the glint of metal under silk. *I don't think he ever takes it off.*

Lana jumped in. *Not necessarily. If he's wearing it, it means he values it more than his own safety. We just have to make him want to show it off. If we can get him in a position where his guard's down—*

He's a vampire in his own lair, Callista cut in. *His guard is never down.*

The bond buzzed with low-level argument. Lana and Connor volleying ideas, Callista shooting holes in them, Mia offering pieces of logistics.

Finally, I cut across them all. *I can make this right. If I can get the crown, all we'll have to do is take the goblet.*

Connor's voice intensified. *Taking the goblet from James isn't exactly an afterthought. That's suicide.*

Not if we plan it, Lana countered. *But the crown comes first.*

Erin, you need to get closer to Malachai without making him suspicious.

Any suggestions?

Play his game, Lana said. *Let him think he's winning. Let him think you're harmless, that you're softening.*

The idea turned my stomach. *You want me to pretend to be grateful to him? To sit here while he—*

While he keeps the crown within reach, she interrupted. *Yes. Because if he realizes you're a threat, we lose our shot.*

Connor jumped in. *If you can figure out when he's most distracted—feeding, bragging, whatever—you signal us through the bond. We'll be ready.*

And then what? I asked. *Even if you come here, how do you get the crown without bringing the entire coven down on you?*

Callista answered this time. *You don't. You let us draw them off. You slip out with the crown while they're focused on us.*

Did one of you mention suicide?

Hope, risk, it's all the same, isn't it? Destin teased. At least he could laugh about it.

Erin, for now, survive, Mia said. *Watch him. Watch the crown. If there's a pattern, find it.*

The bond began to loosen, each of them pulling back into their own bodies, their own worries. But before she left, Lana's voice brushed against mine again. *We'll get you out. And we'll get the crown.*

When her presence faded, I was left alone in the silence of my room, my wolf still lurking in the shadows of my mind.

You could make this easier, I told her.

She made a ripple that felt more like shame than defiance. But still—no words.

CHAPTER
TWENTY-FOUR

Erin

The next day, I paced in my room, unable to settle, the silk hem of Malachai's dress swishing around my legs. The air was annoyingly thick with the rosewater and clove from the bath earlier.

You're thinking about him, my wolf murmured.

I froze, fingers tightening on the carved post of the bed. *Gabriel?*

A pause. Then, *Yes.*

The truth of it hummed under my skin, the low, thrumming ache that had been gnawing at me since I'd woken from the dream. How could I not be thinking of him? I'd experienced him—felt him in and around my body—through dreams, through memories.

Had I thought of him before I knew? Would it mean something if I had?

He's bound to the Shadow Realm, I reminded her, not fully knowing what that meant.

Bound because of me, she whispered, and this time there was only grief.

I treaded carefully. *What do you mean?*

I breathed a sigh of relief as she finally gave in. *Thank you,* I whispered as sight and sound dropped away, replaced by a sudden rush of cold, clean mountain wind and the sharp tang of pine sap. My boots crunched over frozen ground, though I wasn't moving of my own accord. The vision, memory, pulled me forward.

We stood in a clearing under a sky bruised with twilight. Snow clung to the edges of dark stone walls where we stood.

Gabriel and I—Seraphina.

My breath quickened. My wolf's heartbeat thudded in my ears as if the two of us were fused completely in this moment. I drank Gabriel in—the breadth of his shoulders, his bare forearms dusted with snow as he tightened the leather straps on his bracers. His hair was damp from training, curling against his neck.

"You're sure about this?" he asked.

I smiled. "I've never been more sure."

My wolf's emotions tangled with my own in the real world —desire, pride, bone-deep sorrow. I wanted to call out to both of them, to tell them not to do this, but I was only a passenger. I slipped back into Seraphina.

Gabriel stepped closer, his face drawn. "There will be another cost."

"I know. The amulet will bind the light to the Shadow Pack. It will keep the darkness from swallowing us whole."

He reached up, cupping my cheek, and for a moment it was just two people in love—two people who'd fought side by side, who'd bled for the same cause. "I'd rather lose the war than lose you."

I kissed him, then went to work. I set the amulet on the altar we'd built and moved through the runes. We'd done this four times already, and each time it grew easier.

A gust of wind ripped between them, cold enough to bite through leather and steel. Above, the clouds churned, the sky a warning.

My breath hitched, not from the wind but from the voice curling through it. Yes. *Tell me the cost. I will pay it.* I held my hands high and waited.

A mate.

The words knocked the air from my lungs. Had I misheard? "I don't understand—"

Magic does not bargain. A mate is the cost of what you seek.

Gabriel stiffened. He'd heard it too. His hand dropped from my cheek, curling into a fist at his side. "No."

The air thickened, the runes glowing brighter, each stroke of carved stone bleeding light. A circle around the altar flared silver, trapping them inside.

"No," Gabriel said again, louder now, defiant against the storm, his voice nearly lost to the howl of the wind. He turned on the runes like he could break them apart with his bare hands. "There has to be another way."

"There isn't." My voice was steady. I'd read the texts, translated the old tongue, traced every faded line of prophecy and warning. The relics demanded balance. To anchor power like this, something of equal weight had to be surrendered. And the bond between mates . . . there was nothing heavier. Nothing purer.

My mother wouldn't let me keep him. I knew it. It was why we'd been hiding, why we snuck away in the dark. When she found out, she would have him killed.

"Seraphina, please—"

Lightning split the sky, so close the air scorched. I stepped toward him, the circle's light searing the edges of my gown, my hair whipping across my face. "If we don't finish this, Gabriel, the darkness will take everything. The packs. The land. You."

"I don't care." His voice broke on the last word, raw with desperation. "I can fight without it. I will fight without it. But I will not—" He swallowed, jaw locking. "—I will not lose what we have to some ancient magic."

The wind roared, rattling the altar. I lifted my hands, fingers trembling as I traced the air, runes flaring to life beneath my touch. Each one etched itself into light, hanging between them like stars, binding together in an intricate lattice that wrapped around the amulet. The magic's hum deepened into a growl.

Gabriel caught my wrist. "Seraphina—"

I met his eyes. "I won't give you up!" The magic hissed in my ears, its demand turning sharper, angrier. *A mate.*

Terror flashed in his features. "You don't have a choice! If that's the cost—if that's what you want, you know I'll pay it—"

But I shook my head, my decision already made. "I won't give you up. But they will fall, Gabriel. And I will not be the one who lets that happen."

He gripped my shoulders, shaking me, as if he could rattle the thoughts free. "Seraphina!"

The altar cracked down the center, light pouring from within, the amulet's hum reaching a fever pitch. My runes burned hotter, searing my palms, the scent of scorched skin rising. I drew in the magic, pulling it through my veins, letting it braid into my life force.

The voice came again, like the sky itself was speaking. *A mate.*

My heart pounded as I answered, "I am a mate! Take me!"

And before Gabriel could stop me—before he could even realize what I meant—I turned my hand, pressed it to my chest, and whispered the final incantation.

The wind died.

Then the world shattered.

Light exploded from my body, blinding, searing. Gabriel staggered back, the force of it stealing the air from his lungs. The circle flared once, twice, then collapsed inward, funneling everything—Seraphina's essence, her wolf, her soul—into the waiting amulet. The silver flared white-hot, the runes wrapping it sealing into place like molten chains.

I now hovered above them, watching the scene from the sky. Gabriel roared her name, lunging for her, but his hands passed through light and ash. She was dissolving, every thread of her unspooling into the relic.

"No—no, stay with me!" He reached into the light, but it sent him reeling back.

Her voice came softly, carried by the remnants of the wind. "Save them, Gabriel. Live."

And then she was gone.

The storm broke with her. Clouds scattered, the air settling into an eerie stillness. The altar stood cracked, the amulet lying at its center.

Gabriel fell to his knees, weeping.

Paid in full.

My bedroom faded back into existence, where I crouched on all fours, choking for breath. All this time, I'd thought she'd killed him to make the relic. That she'd chosen magic over love. But she'd chosen him. She'd chosen the pack.

Now you understand, my wolf murmured. Her voice was thick, aching. *I left him to bear the weight alone.*

I pushed up from the floor and sank onto the edge of the

bed, my hands trembling against my knees. I couldn't shake the image of Gabriel's face in that moment—raw grief, unshielded, a wound that had never healed. And I couldn't shake the weight in my own chest, the knowledge that he looked at me now and saw her.

He saw the mate he'd lost. Saw the choice she'd made to let him live.

I pressed my palms over my eyes, trying to shut it all out.

I still sat there, the echo of Seraphina's final breath rattling around in my skull, when a faint pull tugged at the back of my mind.

Erin. Lana's voice slid through the bond, low but urgent. *I've been going through the old records again. Trying to figure out who that wolf was in the Shadow Realm. I can't stop thinking about it—what it means. It had to be one of the shadow warriors.*

My stomach tightened. The memory of Gabriel's hands on Seraphina—on me—was still raw, the image carved into my ribs.

Yes. It was Gabriel, I blurted. I was done with secrets.

Silence. Then, *You're sure?*

My wolf. She knew him.

The bond went quiet again, and for a second I thought she'd dropped away. But then her voice came back, slow and careful. *How did she know him?*

I exhaled and fell back on the bed, then let the story tumble out of me. When I finished, Lana let out a slow, *Holy shit.*

Yeah. That about sums it up. My mind still spun with questions. Why was he there in the Shadow Realm? If Seraphina had let him live, wouldn't he have died like we all did?

Hold on, I found something in the book. About shadow warriors.

My pulse picked up. *What did it say?*

Let me check my notes . . . Okay, they were created for one purpose—to protect the Shadow Pack. They swore an oath bound with magic. It says 'a promise was fulfilled.' That magic ties them to the Shadow Realm permanently.

I swallowed hard. *Permanently.*

They can't leave, Lana said. *Not without breaking the oath—and the magic won't let them. They're solitary. Bound to their promise. And to the magic itself.*

The words sank into me like stones into deep water. I thought of Gabriel on the training field, alive and laughing, his hands warm on Seraphina's skin. Then I thought of him now.

So even if— I stopped myself.

Even if they were mated, Lana finished for me anyway, her tone softening. *It wouldn't matter. Not unless something changed in the magic itself.*

I pressed my nails into my palms, willing myself not to let the ache show through the bond.

Tell her I'm sorry. And thank you for confiding in me.

I didn't trust myself to speak.

Lana's presence thinned in the bond. The connection eventually faded, leaving the room too quiet. I sat there in the low lamplight, staring at nothing.

You knew. You knew what he was.

My wolf lowered her head, dropping to the ground. *I knew what he did. I asked him to protect them. He made the promise, and he will never break it. That's why I love him.*

CHAPTER
TWENTY-FIVE

I did everything I could to not dream.

Sleep became something to fear, not something to crave. I'd mastered the art of falling into unconsciousness with my body locked in exhaustion, but my mind fixed on the kind of empty nothing that shut the dreamworld out. No wolves sniffing each other out in some twilight meadow. No old stone barracks and Gabriel's hands on my skin. No memory of Seraphina sacrificing herself for the amulet.

Because if I dreamt, he might be there. And I wasn't sure I could face him again. Not when I now knew exactly what loving me would cost both of us.

But the waking world wasn't much kinder. Malachai bled me again and again in front of the coven. Always the same stage. All dark velvet and black marble. I was displayed under their hunger like an offering at a feast, my pulse loud in the silence before the prick of his needle. He never let them drink, never let my blood serve any purpose other than to taunt them into frenzy and remind them exactly who I was to them—untouchable, except by his hand.

The first few times, I kept my eyes on the floor, jaw locked, teeth aching from the pressure. But then I learned to look. To meet their gaze as they trembled with want. To watch the twitch of fingers that wanted to grab and the flinch as they remembered his warning. It gave me an edge, however thin.

I'd need it.

Because between the performances, I worked on something else. I learned to smile at Malachai. Not the wide, careless grin I gave my pack. This was something quieter, a little guarded, as though it cost me to let him see it. I laughed at the right moments, leaned in when he spoke, dropped my eyes when I knew he wanted to feel powerful. I let him think I was bending.

I was watching him. Always.

It took four days before I witnessed him removing the crown.

It happened in his chambers, and I only caught it because I'd passed by at the wrong—or exactly right—moment. The door wasn't shut, just cracked. I'd learned not to linger too long in one place, but I risked a glance inside.

The room smelled of copper and incense, heady enough to sting the back of my throat. His human attendants, two women and a man, were kneeling before him, skin slick with sweat, their backs marked with fresh lashes. He was bare-chested, silk robe loose and open, the crown lying on a low altar beside him.

Malachai's eyes were closed, his hand resting lightly on the head of one of the women. She was weeping, not in pain, I realized, but in something else entirely. Her mouth hung open, her body trembling, and the sound that escaped her was . . . pleasure.

I swallowed the bile rising in my throat. The other two watched, waiting their turn. Oily black slid through my veins, and I didn't stay long, just enough to sear the image into my mind. Enough to understand what I had to do.

Meanwhile, through the bond, Lana's determination was like a wire strung tight. She didn't waste time with pleasantries, just updates. *I'm working on strengthening the wards around the perimeter. If we can keep them stronger, James may not feel when you enter. It can give us a window.*

What kind of window? I asked.

Minutes. Maybe less.

The bond would go quiet, her focus shifting back to whatever spells and protective circles she was weaving. She'd admitted to working with the witch in the wood. Rowan knew her and trusted her. After seeing what Seraphina had done, I had no doubt she could work magic. I wasn't so sure it would help.

By the seventh night, I finally told Lana what needed to happen. If I could get into that room during the moment I'd seen through the door, I could be close enough to take the crown. Which meant I had to be the one kneeling before him.

This is madness, my wolf muttered the second I slipped back to my own room.

It's the only way.

She didn't argue right away, and that was almost worse than her usual biting sarcasm. We both knew how dangerous this was.

The weekend became a game of positioning. I made sure Malachai noticed my glances, the way I lingered a half-second longer when he passed. Not overt, not enough to tip my hand too soon. Just enough for him to start wondering if his pet was becoming willing.

One night I lay in bed staring at the ceiling, the shadows shifting with the flicker of candlelight, my pulse heavy in my ears.

He'll never believe you're offering yourself, my wolf said finally.

Then I'll make him believe it.

She huffed, a sound halfway between disapproval and reluctant admiration. *And if you fail?*

Then I hope you're ready to take control and tear him apart.

That, at least, earned a growl of approval.

The next evening, after another round of public bleeding, I let my hand linger on his arm as he escorted me from the stage. Just a breath of contact, enough to make him look at me sharply.

"I've been thinking." I let my voice drop low enough for only him to hear. "About . . . how I might serve you better."

His gaze sharpened, a slow smile tugging at his mouth. "Better?"

I flicked my gaze to the woman at his side. "If you'll allow me."

His pupils dilated. "You're jealous. Of the attention I give the others."

My cheeks flushed, and I swallowed hard. "A little."

His mouth curled. "But our deal—"

"I don't care about the deal. The way I live here—I want it to last. You said sometimes you waited a hundred years . . . "

Malachai's lips parted. "You were listening."

"I always listen when you speak."

He didn't answer right away, and I didn't dare fill the silence. When he finally spoke, it was with a note of smug amusement. "We'll see."

As I was preparing for bed, he sent for me.

The attendants bathed me again, brushed my hair until it gleamed, dressed me in silk the color of deep wine. They left my feet bare, my throat bare too—no jewels, no distractions. The scent of rose and myrrh clung to my skin.

When I entered his chambers this time, there was no cracked door. He'd left it wide open, as though daring me to turn back. The air was thick with incense, the same copper tang underlying it. The three humans were there again, kneeling, their eyes downcast.

He sat on the low couch beside the altar with only a swathe of fabric around his waist. The crown lay within arm's reach, its spikes catching the candlelight.

"Come," he said.

My pulse thudded in my ears as I crossed the room. I didn't let my gaze linger on the crown.

I stood in front of him, awaiting his command. He flicked his finger, and I knelt where the others had knelt before me. The stone floor was cold beneath the thin fabric.

Malachai's fingers brushed my jaw, tilting my head up until I met his eyes. "You've been watching me."

"Yes." I didn't bother to deny it.

"And now you want to *please* me."

The word curled in the air between us, part challenge, part promise. I let the silence stretch before I nodded, letting him believe I was ashamed.

His smile deepened. "Don't worry. I'll make this easy for you. Do exactly as I tell you." He crouched down and licked the lobe of my ear. "Unless you'd rather not."

My wolf shuddered.

I know.

Malachai rose, and the first command he gave was simple —pour wine into his cup. My hands were steady, though every nerve in me screamed to stand and race back to the hall.

The second command—feed him a slice of pomegranate. The juice bled over my fingers, staining them red. His gaze followed the drip of juice over my wrist.

He dismissed the other attendants one by one, until it was only the two of us in the room. Then he leaned back, the fabric slipping on his hips. "Kneel closer now."

I moved, my breath catching. My fingers brushed the edge of his feet.

Lana, I hissed.

Here, she answered.

This was it.

I just had to survive whatever came next.

TWENTY-SIX

Gabriel

Erin knelt before the vampire, silk skimming her thighs, candlelight licking her skin. Hunger twisted Malachai's features, and my wolf lunged. I could go to her. That look was enough—she wasn't safe there.

It didn't take much to convince me. I drove forward, but as the veil thinned, a fist hooked my collarbone and wrenched me backward.

The Realm snapped hard. I grunted as I hit the ground, then scrambled to get up and fight, only to freeze mid-crouch.

Lana stood planted in front of me, her expression icy. "Are you out of your damn mind?" The question whipped across the blackness.

"She's within his reach," I growled. "A heartbeat more and—"

"And you were about to blow a hole in our only cover?" She

planted her hands on her hips. "He might've felt you. You lit a signal fire on top of their den."

My wolf prowled at the edge of my skin, shoulders bunched, ready to break past her and run. *Ours. Protect.*

"She bleeds for a spectacle. He wastes it on marble while they starve. You call that a plan?"

"I call it bait." Lana's tone didn't rise. That made it worse. "Your presence turned the water red."

"James only moves by energy. He hunts traces, not—"

"Not what?" She cut me off with a sharp shake of her head. "He knows you exist now. Not just a rumor. A signature. Do you understand what that means? He'll sharpen himself on you. He'll start looking for the seams you guard."

I opened my mouth, then closed it. She was right, but I couldn't shake the image of Erin on her knees out of my head. "Say what you came to say."

She didn't blink. "Your job is to protect. Not to claim. Not to linger. Not to bleed feelings into a battlefield." She took a step closer, chin up. "You don't get the girl, Gabriel. You get the watch."

The line landed like a blow to the gut. My wolf went still.

"She's Seraphina and not," Lana went on, softer now. "That ache in you—honor it on your own time. Not when the pack's life rides on quiet steps." Wind raked the plain, tugging at her hair.

"James." I forced the name out. "Where is he now?"

Lana shrugged. "The more noise we make, the easier the river carries him."

My hands closed, leather biting palm. "If he touches her—"

"You will not intervene."

My wolf answered with a low, steady growl. "Say that again."

"You will not. Intervene." She didn't raise her voice. "Not

unless a throat opens and breath fails. Your oath is clear. You break it, you give him exactly what he wants: proof there are still warriors to corner. He will hunt you first to cut us off from our shield."

"I am not a shield." Heat crept up my spine. "I end anything that reaches for you—any of you."

"Be the wall then," she said. "Walls don't chase. Walls don't telegraph. Walls hold."

I stared past her at the moving horizon, struggling to breathe.

Lana exhaled, some of the fight leaving her shoulders. "We've tightened the wards. I can damp the crown's bleed for a breath or two when it's in the realm. Erin is working him carefully. I don't have much time. I need to help her."

Lana turned to go. "You'll make sure the shadows bend around me while I work. You'll make sure James follows me and not her if he spikes the current. You'll make sure your brothers hold the line at the ripple."

"Brama and Ansel will hold. They always do."

"She can't feel you," Lana added, eyes steady on mine. "Not anymore. Your touch scrapes old wounds open. You know it. She knows it. You go in and you risk the whole table flipping."

The old oath cinched tighter across my ribs. Seraphina's last breath stirred embers I never let show.

"You want me broken," I said.

"I want you brutal and precise." Lana's voice gentled. "You exist where we can't. You move where we would drown. You care about her. Good. Aim it like a blade, not like a torch."

Silence stretched. The Realm listened again, the way it always had to those who could stomach it. My wolf pressed his forehead to the inside of my chest, a slow, grieving lean. "If the pack is in danger, I go."

Another gust. Lana's hair lifted, settled. "If the pack is in danger, *I* go," she said. "I'm the one he doesn't see yet. That's the only advantage I have left. You're the last resort, Gabriel, not the first."

I gave a sardonic laugh. "You lecture a soldier on triage."

"I remind a mate that the battlefield doesn't care about his heart." She flinched, just a ghost of movement, like the word had cut her too. "She can't be yours. Not here. Not now."

"She'll hate you for not running in when it hurts," Lana said. "You'll hate yourself. Welcome to leadership."

"You lecture well," I said dryly.

"It's not a lecture." Her mouth flattened. "It's the only way we all walk out."

TWENTY-SEVEN

Erin

"Closer," Malachai murmured.

I slid my knees over the stone a second time, my heart galloping in my chest.

He reached out and tipped my chin. "You understand the language of patience, little wolf?"

"Teach me." I let a breath of a smile touch my mouth.

His eyes glazed, then he handed me a match and struck it. "You will hold this on my skin. Anywhere you like." He grinned at the expression on my face. "Don't worry, love. I heal as fast as you do. By the end, we'll both do much more damage than this."

I swallowed hard and took the match from his fingers. Malachai stretched in his chair, tipping his head back in complete submission. I started with his fingertip, letting the flame dance."

"Mm. More."

I held the flame closer, flinching as he hissed through his teeth. Malachai reached out and placed my hand on the flat of his stomach. "Comfort me."

I dragged my nails lightly over his skin, moving the flame to the next finger. His breathing quickened. He waited until the flame burned out, then lifted his head. "Your turn."

He gripped my wrist and lifted me from the floor, walking me over to the bed. "Lie down." I did as he asked. He took the burnt out match from my fingers. "Have you ever enjoyed pain before?"

I shook my head. *Lana, hurry the hell up.*

Malachai prowled closer. "Then I will start small." His face grew somber, almost childlike. "Thank you for letting me be the first—the one to take your innocence."

I closed my eyes and let him believe it was in anticipation while I did my best not to throw up. He dragged his fingers over my skin until he reached my hair, then curled his fingers and pulled.

I gasped.

"Shh," he purred, releasing the tug. "I shall do it again, but I will comfort you as you did me." His other hand brushed my ankle, then slid up my calf, lingered at the inside of my knee, and continued upward under the hem of my dress.

Lana—

The club's music wobbled, bass turning to a subsonic grind that made me wince. A new sound slid underneath, so high it wasn't sound at all, but pressure.

Malachai flew back, slamming his palms to his ears.

A thud hit the door. Then two more. He stumbled forward, but could barely move with the pain in his head. He looked back at me. "Do not move!"

"I won't." I made myself small, playing the scared little girl he wanted me to be.

Cloud him with hunger, Lana spoke into my head.

I searched the bed, the nightstand, and found the needle he used on me each night. The sound stopped, and Malachai dropped his hands, gasping for breath. Before he could recover, I grabbed the sharp metal and pricked my skin. Over and over. The blood beaded, and he swung toward me, eyes wild.

I brought my wrist to my lips and licked, slow enough for heat to rise in my skin and his gaze to catch on the movement. Every instinct rebelled. I swallowed revulsion and kept the performance private to only to the predator in him.

He crossed the room without looking away from my mouth. He grabbed my wrist with a desperate snarl, and as he lowered his head, the club detonated.

Not sound this time, light. Every lamp below flared as if a match had been struck in every corner at once, then snapped off. On, off, on—stuttering bright-white pulses that turned the lair into a throat of lightning. Strobe. *They felt everything more intensely.*

Malachai dropped to the floor, squeezing his eyes closed. That's when I bolted. I jumped from the bed, ran to the crown and grabbed it, then darted for the door.

The corridor beyond the arch swelled with heat and perfume. Lamps strobed through the club. My bare feet skidded on polished wood, the crown's spikes biting my skin through silk. Everything in me screamed. *Left,* my wolf barked. *Kitchen hall, then stairs, then the service door. Go.*

The service stairs pitched into shadow. A crash thundered behind me, Malachai slamming into the doorframe, and a flood of footsteps burst after. I leapt three steps at a time, hip cracking the rail, breath punching from my lungs. The crown weighed more than I expected. It dragged.

At the first landing, a vampire appeared, one of the attendants. She moved fast, but a shape hit her from the side. Destin, all shoulders and momentum. He took her into the wall without a sound, palm over her mouth, wrist twisted. She sagged.

"Move," he breathed, and his body was already between me and the stairwell, a wedge to slow what followed.

I vaulted past, crown hugged tight, silk riding indecently high on my thighs. The door exploded inward. Connor filled the frame, shoulders broader than the opening, soot on his cheek like a war stripe. He grabbed the crown-hand wrist and swung me behind him in the same motion. "Got you."

Two vampires hit him at once. He met them like a battering ram, catching one by the throat and slamming him into the doorjamb hard enough to crater the wood. The other went for my shoulder. I ducked, crown spikes grazing her midriff. She recoiled as if stung.

Mia appeared and flanked us. We spilled into a service corridor humming with dead fluorescent lights. The world pitched between brightness and blackout as the strobe bled through wherever doors didn't seal. The glamour Malachai wrapped this place in had ripped, the club's architecture showed its bones—concrete, cinderblock, utility pipes that rattled under the sound system's death throes.

Lana waited at the far end with a door cracked to the field behind the house. Sweat beaded her temple, but she grinned when she saw us.

Night hit like a slap. We raced through the dead cornfield, then Destin led us to the street.

"Truck," Connor snapped. When he arrived at the place they'd left it, we piled in—Destin at the wheel, the rest of us a tangle of limbs filling the other seats.

Gravel spat under tires as we peeled onto a side street, then a back road that cut between shuttered shops and sleeping houses. Destin drove like a man who knew every pothole by name. The town fell away. Forest swallowed the edges.

"Talk," Lana said, front passenger seat, eyes on the mirror, voice even. "Crown?"

"Here." My hands didn't loosen.

"Good," she said. "Sorry about the disco. The amps almost cooked me."

"That was you?" Connor asked, half-admiration, half-reproach.

"Borrowed the DJ's board," Lana said. "And the fire alarm. And the emergency lights. And the old municipal siren circuit no one's fixed since the '90s."

A laugh cracked out of me. "Smart."

"Smarter if we're not dead." She finally looked back at me. "You okay?"

My throat worked once. "Yes."

Mia's knee pressed against mine. Warm. Steady. The only thing in me that didn't jolt at touch. "You did it." The pride in her words almost undid me.

Gratitude hit like a hot flash. They had stepped into a vampire's den for me. For this. For all of us. I gripped Mia's hand hard.

We turned down a rutted dirt road. Destin killed the headlights two bends in. The truck drifted forward on muscle memory.

"Half a kilometer," Lana said. "Ripple's fresh."

We stopped where the forest opened into a thin stand of alder.

"You found another one?" I asked.

Lana nodded.

I climbed out, legs unsteady. *Quick,* my wolf urged, nose lifted, ears pinned. *In and out.*

Mia pressed a small bottle into my palm. The sleeping pill clinked inside. "A quarter," she whispered. "You don't need the full dose. You're dead on your feet."

I dry-swallowed. The chalk stuck on my tongue. Lana stepped into my space, pressing her brow to mine for a heartbeat, old comfort, old trust. "We'll do the book first since we're still protected here. I'll find it. Seal it fast. If he feels it, he'll shove back."

Lana prepared to enter the Shadow Realm, and she read the worry all over my face.

"Don't worry. I have protections there."

Gabriel? I asked, just between the two of us.

She nodded. "He knows his place now. He won't be showing up unexpectedly."

The breath whooshed from my lungs as she turned, and relief flooded my veins. Lana. She was the reason he hadn't come in Malachai's room. My wolf's tongue *lolled* with contentment. I hadn't seen that in years.

I lay down in the cold leaves. The crown rested on my abdomen, heavy enough to bruise. The pill tugged. Breath lengthened. The ripple leaned down as if to smell me. Then everything slid.

I waited for Lana. She was there faster than I could count to twenty. The book must've been close. As soon as I had it, dark swallowed light in one slow pour. The ground unhooked from the idea of ground. Stars blinked out like someone pinched them.

Nothing. No temperature. No wind. No weight. Only a pressure, everywhere and nowhere, like being inside a held note.

BACK AGAIN.

. . .

IMAGES, because words always failed here. Plus, the magic recognized me. It knew what I wanted. I showed the book.

PAYMENT?

MY MIND SCRAMBLED. I worked to think of anything I could sacrifice, but the magic wasn't waiting this time.

In an instant, my tongue dried up. Taste vanished. Not pain. An erasure. The memory of sweetness went blank. Salt blinked out. Metal disappeared from my tongue like a language forgotten overnight. Panic kicked in.

No. I didn't want to offer that, but what else could I give?

I pushed the book into the black. It fell without falling, sank without motion, left my hands with a tug-pop like a cork releasing. A seam closed. Pressure eased.

The upward slide returned me to cold leaves and breath that hurt going in. Eyes opened. Tree branches sketched themselves across a pale slice of sky. Sound returned in layers—my name hissed at a whisper, the rustle of coats, the tick of a cooling engine.

Mia's face hovered above mine. "Hey. Hey, you with me?"

Her jacket smelled like her when she pulled it tighter around me. I nodded once. No words.

Lana crouched at my side. "Did it take?"

My hands were empty. I nodded. "Yes. The book is sealed."

TWENTY-EIGHT

We spent three days at a seedy hotel in Terrace. I barely slept. I couldn't stop thinking about Gabriel. How he'd come to my room and then left. I hadn't seen him since.

He didn't come when I sealed the crown. I couldn't end up in the dreamworld and not see him a second time.

Why did I miss him so much?

I searched for an answer to that. Every argument I gave myself refused to hold water. We were friends. We shared secrets. He made me feel safe. He was strong, but I didn't fear him. Most terrifying . . . I trusted him. When he didn't show up, it hurt.

That third morning, dawn skimmed the spruce tips with silver, the kind that made frost look like sugar dusted over needles. We kept to the fringe where the town thinned into cutblock and alder scrub.

Lana took us back to the same ripple. We didn't have time to drive back to Kitimat.

I took my half pill. My head grew thick, and the ripple shimmered around me, warm as breath, pulling me into its endless current. I floated on the edge of it, my mind reaching for the now familiar thread. *Almost,* I told myself. Just a few more seconds, and we'd have the crown sealed before anyone knew we'd been here.

But the moment before I could fully sink into the magic, something hooked me hard, wrenching me backward through the threads. The ripple tore away from me in a dizzy rush, and I slammed into the cold air of the real world.

I barely had time to gasp before a hand clamped around my arm. A sharp sting pierced my skin. The rush of something chemical burned through my veins, heavy and cloying. For a breath, I thought I'd drop, thought the world would collapse into darkness.

Then the darkness fled. It was like fire washing through my head, scorching the edges of my thoughts, tearing the sleep from my body in an instant. My eyes snapped open. My heart slammed against my ribs.

James smiled above me, the kind of smile that didn't bother hiding its cruelty. "Did you really think I wouldn't be ready for you?"

Behind him, a figure moved from the forest. Malachai strode toward us, his boots grinding against the frost-hardened ground. His eyes glinted.

Mia, Connor, and Destin were already moving. It was obvious by the fact that Destin had already shifted and Mia had blood on her shoulder that they'd already tried once.

They came in fast and fierce, Mia with a flash of teeth,

Connor with a low, lethal blur, Destin a storm of raw force, but it was like trying to hold back the tide with bare hands. James swept Connor aside with a burst of shadow-strength that sent him crashing into the dirt. Malachai caught Mia by the throat and flung her back into Destin, knocking both of them to the ground.

"You've wasted enough time," Malachai growled, turning his attention to the relic lying between us.

The crown. Its dark gold gleamed, carved with symbols that shifted under the light. I reached for it, but Malachai slapped my hand away and took it himself.

"Give it to me," James said smoothly, extending a hand. "And she's yours." The words sliced through me.

Malachai tilted his head, gaze flicking between James and me. His lips curled, revealing just the edge of a fang. "My patience has been worthwhile." He took a step, but a blur of motion crashed into him, hard enough to drive him back.

Gabriel.

My heart leaped. His wolf hit Malachai again like a hammer, driving him into the ground. They rolled, Gabriel's claws flashing, both of their teeth bared. Malachai was fast, and Gabriel wasn't working with the advantage of surprise. Every blow Malachai landed drew a yip or grunt from Gabriel, but he didn't slow. He fought like a wolf who had nothing left to lose.

The fight was vicious, desperate. Malachai nearly got his teeth to Gabriel's throat twice, but each time Gabriel twisted free, countering with a strike meant to break bone. Finally, with a roar that tore through the clearing, Gabriel drove his claws deep into Malachai's chest. The vampire's body went rigid, a strangled sound tearing from his mouth. Then Gabriel wrenched his arm free and stabbed again, then once more.

Malachai crumpled, lifeless, into the dirt. Silence held for one breath. Two. Finally, his body turned to ash.

I nearly wept with relief. But this wasn't over. Gabriel stumbled back, searching for James, then reached with a paw for the crown. As soon as he made contact, the air split.

The shadows didn't crawl. They struck. The trees shivered, their branches groaning. Black boiled up from the ground like flood water, and somewhere deep inside me, my wolf screamed. *No!*

Lana ran toward us, hair wild, eyes wide. But she was too late. The shadows surged, curling around the crown in Gabriel's hands, pouring into him, pouring into the world. The bond between the relics flared like molten metal. I felt it as clearly as my own heartbeat. They had been sleeping—dormant—and now they were wide awake.

Selfish act, my wolf snarled in my head, the sound more rage than fear. *The relics know. They remember.*

The words weren't just for me. They rang out across the pack bonds, shoving into every mind tied to the Shadow Pack. A warning. A curse. A truth.

My knees buckled under the weight of it. I clutched my head as visions struck—flickers of the dagger, the amulet, the book, all stirring like predators scenting blood. Gabriel's eyes met mine, shock and dawning horror tangled in his expression. He'd done it to save me. And in saving me, he'd activated the exact power the relics protected against.

CHAPTER
TWENTY-NINE

The relics knew.

Lana was shouting something, but I couldn't hear her. My wolf was being dragged back to the shadow realm, and I couldn't hold much longer.

Erin's hand went to her chest. Her pulse jumped under her skin, too fast, too hard. What was happening? I had to get to her. To figure out what I could do to stop this.

Branches broke from the trees and what looked like a sharpened spear tore through Destin's left thigh.

Lana screamed and Mia fought the wind with her to get to him, but Connor's head snapped toward Erin like a wolf catching a scent it couldn't ignore.

No. The amulet.

They'd both bonded with it, and now it was calling to

them. Erin staggered, eyes glazed but not unfocused—they were locked on something I couldn't see.

The pack couldn't help. I shifted back, not caring whether I had clothes or not. "Erin!" My voice cracked like a whip. No response.

They both moved in separate arcs, almost a mirror of each other, slipping between the trees. I stumbled forward, chasing after her. "Erin!"

When I finally blocked her path, her eyes weren't hers anymore. "Look at me." I caught her shoulders. The heat from her skin was unnatural, fever-bright. "You can fight this—"

Her snarl cut me off. Wolf-deep, unthinking, she shoved me back hard. I pivoted, caught Connor by the arm before he could vanish into the treeline. His lips peeled back over his teeth. The compulsion made him stronger, sharper, less human. His free hand came up to my throat in a move that should have been familiar, but there was no recognition in his eyes.

"Connor, listen—" My fingers dug into pressure points along his wrist, forcing him to loosen his grip. "It's the amulet. It's not you."

He slammed me into a cedar trunk. Bark scraped down my back. Both their wolves pressed at the edges of this moment, desperate to obey the call.

Erin kept walking. I let Connor go and went for her again, grabbing her from behind, locking my arm across her collarbones. "Erin, stop!"

She didn't fight me like an enemy. She fought me like I was a wall between her and oxygen. Every twist of her body, every jerk of her shoulders was designed to *get out*.

Let me go. The words weren't out loud. They were in my head, soft and deadly, her voice but not her will.

"No," I growled, tightening my grip. "Not until you see what's happening."

She bucked hard, breaking my balance. The ground tilted, and we both went down. She was on her feet before I could blink, the compulsion pulling her forward again. Connor was only a few paces behind her now.

I went after them a third time. Wolves are damn stubborn—I am worse—but this wasn't a fight I could win with strength alone. I caught Erin's wrist again, twisted just enough to make her stop. Her head turned toward me, slow, deliberate, unnatural.

"It's not yours," I told her. "You don't belong to it."

Her lip curled, her wolf too close to the surface. "I have to."

"No. You think you do, but you don't."

Her pupils blew wide. For half a heartbeat, I thought I had her. But then Connor's hand closed on her other arm, and the compulsion surged between them like a current. She tore free, and they were gone, weaving into the deeper woods.

I could track them. I could run them down. But the amulet's pull was designed to keep its prey away from anything that might break the hold. I'd already failed once today. I wouldn't risk them both by thinking my will was stronger than that magic.

The truth was acid in my mouth. I needed help.

THIRTY

ERIN

The pull was a living thing. It hooked into the marrow of my bones, threading itself through my nerves until every step forward felt like gravity demanded it.

And then—

Stop.

The word was a snap inside my head, sharp enough to make me stumble. My wolf's voice, low and commanding. The pressure in my chest buckled. The thread tugging me forward frayed, then tore completely, leaving me breathless and blinking in the dim light.

But Connor didn't slow.

I lunged forward, catching his arm. "Connor—wait—"

He wrenched free without even looking at me, his face locked in that blank mask the amulet loved to carve over its prey. "Have to go," he murmured. It wasn't him—it was the relic speaking through him.

"Connor, listen to me!" I grabbed at his sleeve again, digging in my heels. "You're not thinking straight—"

He shoved me off with enough force to send me staggering backward into the trunk of a cedar. Bark bit my palms. He kept walking.

Let him go, my wolf said, not unkindly.

I shook my head hard. *No. He's my pack.*

And right now, he's the amulet's.

I pressed the heel of my hand to my temple, trying to clear the static crawling through my thoughts. "Then tell me how to break it."

You can't. Not unless you take the amulet itself.

My breath caught. *Then that's what we'll do. We take it, we seal it—*

Seal it? She almost laughed, but there was no humor in it. *Do you even know what sealing means, Erin? Do you know what you're doing when you drop a relic into one of those ripples?*

Of course I do. It's what we've been doing—

No. It's what I've been doing. And you've been trusting me without knowing why.

Her voice twisted inside me, thick with something I couldn't name—regret, maybe. Shame.

I forced my breathing to steady. *Then tell me.*

She hesitated, and I realized she was afraid. My wolf—my sharp, bitter, fearless wolf—was *afraid.*

Gabriel saved you, she said instead, voice quieter now. *That's the only reason you're still here.*

The memory of him at the club flashed bright—the cut of his shoulders in the light, the speed and violence of him, the way his eyes had locked on mine like he could drink me in and never be full. My pulse leapt traitorously.

You think about him when you're supposed to be thinking about the relics.

I swallowed. *I can't help it. I don't know when it started, but I* — My throat closed around the word. *I want him. I need him. And I hate that I can't stop.*

Silence. Then her voice softened. *That's the bond. Not just yours. Mine. His. All tangled up in this mess you stepped into the moment you inherited me.*

The trees closed in around us, shadows stretching like fingers across the frost. Connor was farther ahead now, his back disappearing between two thick spruces. I should have run after him. I didn't.

My wolf spoke again. *Erin. The relics created the Shadow Realm.*

The world tilted under me. *That's not—*

It is.

The words dropped into me like stones in deep water, sinking fast, pulling everything else down with them.

I wasn't sure until now, but I can feel it. That same magic that tore me to pieces when I created them. Every piece we made, she went on, *the dagger, the crown, the goblet, the book, the amulet— all of it wasn't meant to trap the darkness. It was meant to hold it. Contain it. But power like that doesn't just sleep. It changes the space around it. Twists it. The Shadow Realm wasn't some ancient curse we stumbled into.*

Her shame burned hotter than the compulsion had, scalding my thoughts.

And you lost everything for it, I whispered.

I did. I lost him. I lost my pack. I lost myself. And for what? Look at it. Every inch of it has been used for more evil than good. Every sacrifice I made fed the same darkness I thought I was fighting.

I clenched my fists, nails biting my palms. Connor vanished fully from sight. I didn't follow. Not yet. Because for the first time since I'd taken on this fight, I wasn't sure what winning even looked like anymore.

What did we know? The relics couldn't be used selfishly without damaging the person wielding them. I'd seen it. Malachai with his crown, twisted by hunger and power. James with the goblet, stronger but more corrupted each time he used it.

And me.

I was linked to the amulet, and . . . I was linked to each one. Because of my wolf. *Seraphina.*

James wanted the relics. Always had. And now, I finally understood why. They weren't just weapons. They were keys. Pieces of a whole. Pieces of something that was never supposed to exist.

I thought sealing them would be enough, that we could lock them away and keep them from being used for evil. But the truth was so much worse. The relics had been used for both purposes, depending entirely on the heart of whoever wielded them. Protection. Destruction. It was all the same magic, all the same source.

The power shouldn't exist.

It hit me like ice water. That was the truth my wolf had been circling, the shame she hadn't wanted to say out loud. The relics held unnatural, stolen power made into something that twisted everyone who touched it.

I looked at Connor, at the way he strained toward the amulet without even realizing he was doing it, the compulsion eating him alive from the inside out. I couldn't keep playing this game—taking relics, sealing them, hoping we'd outwit James. Because even if we won this battle, there would be another and another. The magic wasn't ours to keep.

It had to go back. Not locked in a ripple. Not hidden in some warded vault. Back to wherever Seraphina had pulled it from in the first place. Back into the wild magic it had been stolen from.

Put it back in order.

Give the magic back.

Erin, my wolf murmured, almost wary now. *Do you understand what that means?*

Yes. My pulse was pounding, but my voice inside was steady. *It means we stop fighting to keep it. All of it. Even if it means giving it to James long enough to finish it.*

We will finish what I started.

CHAPTER

THIRTY-ONE

Erin

Connor didn't even hesitate when I told him.

"We have to get back what we sealed," I said. My voice was calm, deliberate, even though the truth of it burned like acid down my throat. "We have to give the relics to James."

His eyes lit, the amulet's pull shimmering in the gold-flecked green of his irises. "Finally." I'd just confirmed the thing he'd been dying to hear.

The truth was, I could feel the amulet clawing at him, warping his will to match its own. But right now, that was an advantage. I needed him to agree without asking too many questions.

We crossed into the Shadow Realm together, my heartbeat drumming in my ears. The air shifted around us, and that's where Gabriel found us. He stepped from the darkness. He'd been waiting, his gaze slashing over Connor before settling on me. His expression was a storm I couldn't read—rage, worry, disbelief. "Erin."

The way he said my name—it landed in my chest and ached.

"What are you doing?" His eyes flicked to Connor again, narrowing. "This isn't right."

I squared my shoulders. "I know exactly what I'm doing."

His hand caught my arm, not rough but unyielding. "You're making a mistake."

Connor moved forward like he was ready to fight him, but I threw an arm out to keep them apart. My voice dropped to a whisper, urgent. "You didn't show yourself to me for a reason."

"I—" He looked at me, confused.

I pulled my arm free from his grip. "You will let me go."

"Erin." He reached for me again, but I backed away.

"It won't be the same," I promised. It was cryptic, and I didn't explain. I couldn't. If James even caught a hint of what I was doing, it would be over before it started. "Tell the others— tell them to stay away."

Thankfully, he got a piece of the message. Gabriel's jaw worked. But he didn't stop me when I turned away, when Connor and I slipped deeper into the realm.

The nearest ripple shivered before me, a seam in reality catching the light like oil on water.

I stepped forward, and the world peeled open. The magic inside wasn't empty. It was *aware*.

It pressed against my skin, curious, tasting my intent the way a predator tastes the air.

It remembered me. Remembered taking the book from my hands, swallowing it into the endless dark where it couldn't be reached.

. . .

BACK AGAIN.

THIS TIME I didn't wait. *I'm taking it,* I told it, though the words didn't pass my lips. *All of it.*

The magic recoiled, like I'd offended it, then surged forward in a rush so cold my lungs locked. It coiled around my ribs, testing my resolve, trying to push me back.

When I held my ground, it yielded—slipping into me in a rush, hot and cold at once, a tide dragging me under. My wolf arched inside me, her head tipped back in something between a howl and a gasp.

Give up your protection of the book, and I will take my sense of taste.

THE PAYMENT IS ALREADY SPENT.

No. It was an equal exchange. You may take part of it for the service you rendered.

THE MAGIC HISSED, but when the book landed in my hand, I knew this would work. Hope filled my chest.

"Quickly," I said to Connor. "We must retrieve the dagger."

We pushed forward, racing as only one could through the Shadow Realm. I'd forgotten how freeing it was to be here. The feeling only lasted a second because I remembered why I'd avoided this place with my life.

James hadn't appeared yet. He had to be watching.

The next ripple was sharper—its light fractured like shattered glass. The dagger's magic was different, more feral. The moment I touched it, pain lanced through my palms, as if the ripple itself was cutting me open. The magic here had a memory of violence, of every drop it had spilled, and it wanted me to feel each one.

It whispered images—Kael's arm slick with blood, Nathan Black's eyes before he fell, Callista and Lana's skin marred by its mark.

I didn't fight the hurt. I let it in, and the ripple relented. The dagger's power rushed back into me, threading itself through my veins like molten wire. The memory my wolf had given dropped into my head as the cold metal of the dagger hit my palm. My tears pricked with gratitude.

I dropped back into the Shadow Realm next to Connor to find James stepping from the shadows. He saw what he wanted to see. A thief who'd just brought him everything.

And I let him.

CHAPTER
THIRTY-TWO

James stood there with that smug grin. Erin was at his side, the relics heavy in her hands, and for one gut-sick instant, I thought she'd chosen him.

I didn't remember shifting. One heartbeat, I was man, the next I was wolf, the ground tearing under my paws as I launched at him. My claws raked for his throat. The goblet's power burned through him, through the air itself, but I didn't care. All I could see was James, all I could feel was the taste of victory in my teeth if I just—

Something slammed into my side. Not James.

Erin.

Her wolf came at me hard and fast, hitting low and twisting, her weight dragging me away from my target. She snarled, lips peeled back, amber eyes locking on mine with a command I felt in my bones: *Stop.*

I didn't. Couldn't. My rage had teeth, and they were buried too deep. So she bit me. Her jaws closed on my shoulder, not to cripple, but to *hurt*. Sharp enough to cut through the haze, to rip me back into myself.

I stumbled. She released me, breath heaving. *Trust me*, she threw at the bond, and then she shifted.

One heartbeat fur, the next skin. The Shadow Realm clothed her instantly, black fabric winding around her frame.

James watched her, suspicion flickering over his face as she stepped toward him. Then he did exactly what I feared—he gathered the relics. Crown, dagger, book amulet, goblet, all in his hands, their magic bleeding together, the air around him vibrating like it was seconds from splitting open.

Erin didn't move to stop him. Her gaze never left him, but I saw the change—the way her shoulders squared, her breathing steadied, her focus turned inward.

Then her fingers began to trace something in the air. I frowned, watching the movement. It took me longer than I'd like to admit, but understanding finally dawned. I knew that shape. I'd seen it burned into Seraphina's floor a thousand years ago.

My chest tightened. *Trust me.*

She'd broken the compulsion. She wanted James to hold the relics. But why? What could the runes do now that they—

Power rolled out from her in a wave, snapping at the tether James had knotted into the relics. His eyes flashed, his face reddening with the effort of keeping them in his hands.

Then I felt it—her. Her magic. Her *self*. She was pulling it all back, every piece she'd given away, every thread that bound her to the curse. And in the same breath, she was reaching for me.

THIRTY-THREE

ERIN

The last line of the reversed rune burned white across my vision. For a heartbeat, nothing happened. Then everything broke.

The Shadow Realm screamed.

James's smirk faltered, the relics in his grasp shuddering violently as if they'd been torn from the inside out. A jagged light split the darkness, running straight through him—and through the man who'd appeared beside him, the man I'd seen with him in my dream, magic seeker whose hunger for power had matched his own.

I held tight, trying to complete the final curve. For a heartbeat, I thought it might work. Then the magic bucked.

It tore through me like a living thing, too wild to cage, too vast to bend. The relics screamed in James's hands. The air around him split apart, light and shadow colliding with bone-breaking force.

The ground shuddered. My knees hit the dirt. I clung to the rune, but it slipped like water through shaking fingers.

I can't hold it—

You can, my wolf snarled, but there was no hiding the strain in her voice. The magic was too strong, too old. And I was just one soul against the tide.

Then, through the chaos—

Erin.

The pack bond flared, sudden and bright. Lana, Destin, Callista, Mia, Connor—five wolves slamming into my mind, into my soul, their power rushing toward me like a river breaking a dam.

We're here.

One by one, they shoved their wolves forward, bodies braced. The bond between us tightened, and the rune—my failing rune—caught.

We became one pulse.

One voice.

One force.

The magic howled in answer, fighting to throw us off, but it couldn't decide where to strike. We were everywhere. Lana's stubborn fire anchored me. Destin's raw strength braced my spine. Callista's precise, careful energy threaded through the rune's weak points, shoring them up. Mia's light steadied my breath. Connor's unyielding presence locked all of us in place.

I reached for the life I'd stolen from the realm, forcing it back into the cracks, and in doing so reached for the one I'd never been given—mine and Gabriel's. Heat sparked in the tether between us, the faint shimmer of the bond I thought had been lost forever.

It leapt from wolf to wolf, pack to warrior, like fire catching in dry grass. And in that moment, I knew. It wasn't just my wolf's longing—it was mine. I loved him. Not because he'd been hers. Because he had become mine. Because he saw me when no one else did. Because he made me feel safe when I had every reason to run.

I dove into the bond without hesitation, dragging him with me. His shock crackled like lightning, and then his wolf surged up to meet mine—heat, relief, *home.*

The rune flared white-hot, and James's smirk broke as the magic reversed. He and the magic seeker beside him didn't even have time to scream before the light ripped them apart. Dust scattered into the collapsing wind.

The Shadow Realm began to melt. The sky ran like paint into blackness, the ground splitting beneath us. Gabriel staggered. Brama fell to one knee. Ansel dissolved into drifting shadow.

Hold it, I snarled through the bond. *Hold it—*

We poured everything we had into the breaking realm, until there was nothing left but the pack and the bond and the desperate hope that this would be enough.

Gabriel's wolf wrapped around mine in the chaos, the heat of him the only solid thing left.

The ground vanished. The bond stretched—strained—

And then I fell.

CHAPTER

THIRTY-FOUR

GABRIEL

I woke on needles and damp loam, the world lurching in and out of focus like a lantern swinging on a hook.

Cold breath sawed in, and the forest knit itself together around me. Brama groaned to my right, one arm thrown over his face. Ansel lay on his side to my left, coughing up ash that wasn't there anymore.

We wore dark wool, leather bindings, buckles burnished by years, not weeks. A smear of ash shadowed Brama's ja,w and Ansel's hair was braided back with a thong of sinew, just as it had been the first winter we took the oath.

For a blink, the sight knocked the wind from me. We should have been dust. We should have been song.

Alive. My wolf's voice landed with the weight of a hand on my shoulder. *Find her.*

I pushed to my knees. The earth heaved once under my

palms before steadying. No Realm underfoot. No oath pressing the ribs. The old chain still existed, but it lay slack and distant.

Brama propped himself on an elbow, eyes scanning the treeline, then the sky. "What did she do?" His voice scraped like he'd swallowed gravel.

"Broke it," Ansel muttered, head tipped back, eyes closed. "Or mended it. Depends on whether you liked the world as it was."

I stood. Blood roared and steadied. My boots sank half an inch into soft duff. When I shifted weight, the ground gave. A raven heckled from somewhere beyond the mist, three harsh barks. Sound arrived whole, not with that stretched, hollow quality the Shadow had given everything.

I tested the air again. Not a trace of James. No coppery sting of the goblet's wrongness.

Ansel clocked me. "What is it?"

"That," I said, turning east. Pines thinned in that direction; the fog glowed, paler, rising. "Civilization."

Brama rolled to his haunches, joints popping, and fixed the straps on his vambrace by muscle memory. The gesture dragged the mind backward—camp smoke, hammered bronze bowls, horse sweat, a woman's laugh through a tent flap—and snapped it forward again. He looked down at his own clothes, grimaced. "We're dressed for a pageant."

"Or a funeral," Ansel said, levering himself upright.

Move. My wolf pressed, impatient. *Castle. She will go there.*

For a heartbeat, my head filled with limestone walls sun-warmed, flags bright as spilled paint, Seraphina's hand on a parapet catching skirts so she could climb faster to throw her arms around my neck. I shoved the vision aside and ran.

Branches raked leather. Alder lashed my thighs. Spruce tips brushed my shoulders. My lungs opened and took the morning like a draught of cold wine. Brama and Ansel fell in behind, ghost-fast and silent, the way we had moved through winter campaigns.

The fog thinned. Trees thinned. I burst out of the green and landed on . . . asphalt. There were low roofs bristling with frost, a mill's long spine smoking at the far edge, a river throwing pale light as it bent. Power lines stitched the sky. Pickup trucks glinted on a frontage road. A bus sighed at a stop and kneeled, doors hissing. On the near slope, modest houses shouldered together like sheep, woodsmoke trailing thin and white from metal chimneys.

Not a castle. Her town.

Gratitude hit like a blow—unexpected, fierce, knees-weakening. I stood there and let it take me. The world could have spat us anywhere. Backward into the dust of our oath, forward into a dead place that didn't know our names. Instead, it had coughed us onto the edge of *her* world.

Ansel whistled low. "Not the courtyard I expected."

Brama snorted. "Look at him. He thinks he knows the streets."

He was right. I charted the quickest route without thinking —the deer track that became the gravel lot, the chain-link gap kids cut with snips, the gutter that always overflowed in rain. I had paced these lines a thousand nights, eyes pressed to a glass that would not let me through. I started moving before either of them could say another word.

THIRTY-FIVE

Erin

Mia's living room was warm, almost stifling after the damp chill outside, the smell of boiled herbs hanging in the air. I sat on the edge of her worn couch, legs curled under me, while she dabbed a cooling salve along the scrapes on my arms. She clucked under her breath at the deeper cuts, muttering about how many times in the last month she'd patched me back together.

The knock on the door made us both jump. Connor stalked out of the kitchen to open it. When he didn't say anything, my head snapped up.

Connor pulled the door wide. And there he was. Gabriel. Standing there in the same battle gear he wore in the Shadow Realm.

How was it possible? He was alive. Here. And nobody was going for my throat.

My wolf surged, but Mia held me in place. "Not finished yet." She turned to face him. "You'll have to wait. Would you like to take a seat?"

Gabriel kept his eyes locked on mine. He stalked into the room, let Connor close the door, then stood in the corner like a storm held barely in check, his shoulders squared, jaw set hard enough I could see the muscle ticking there.

He's pacing in his head, my wolf said, sharp with recognition. *He will not wait long.*

I almost told her to stop, but the truth was, I could feel it too—the press of him against the room, the way his gaze kept snagging on me, then flicking away like he was afraid to burn through what little restraint he had left.

My skin tingled in anticipation.

"Nothing broken," Mia announced, straightening. "No fever. You need rest, food, and about three days without throwing yourself into anyone's line of fire." She glanced at Gabriel and didn't even bother to pretend she thought I'd listen.

The moment she stepped back, Gabriel moved. No hesitation, no checking to see if I'd protest, just a solid, sure presence sweeping in, lifting me into his arms like I weighed nothing.

"Gabriel—" I started.

"Not here," he said, voice low, final. He carried me out into the gray morning, his stride long and steady. My head rested against his chest, the rhythm of his heartbeat under my ear both too fast and impossibly sure. The air bit at my skin, still raw from everything that had happened, but his arms held me in a pocket of heat.

"I don't live close," I murmured.

"You walked it once."

As if on cue, when we were halfway down the road when a

truck slowed beside us. Liam leaned across the seat, the window rolling down with a squeak. "Erin. Need a ride?"

I nearly laughed out loud. "I'm good this time, thanks."

Liam's eyes flicked to Gabriel, and with a smir,k he drove on.

Gabriel didn't say a word. He just kept walking, each step a quiet, relentless pilgrimage. My wolf pressed close inside me, tail high, pacing like she'd been waiting for this exact moment.

By the time we reached my building, my pulse had settled into the same rhythm as his. He didn't set me down on the steps. Instead, he shifted me slightly, holding me tighter, his chin brushing my hair. "Is it locked?"

I nodded, then fidgeted for my keys. He took them and unlocked the door.

Inside, the air was cooler. My apartment still smelled faintly of the cedar shampoo I'd used the last time I was there. Had it been days? Weeks?

Gabriel finally set me on my feet, but his hands didn't leave me. One arm curved protectively around my back, the other still at my waist, thumb brushing the edge of my hip. For a moment, neither of us spoke. The silence between us was thick, charged.

"I need you to hear me," he said finally. "When you were with Malachai . . . every breath I took was a fight. I wanted to tear him apart for touching you. I wanted to give you—" His jaw tightened, then he pushed on. "I wanted to give you pleasure without pain. Without fear. Without anything that would make you flinch."

Heat curled low in my belly. My wolf prowled forward, ears forward.

"I wanted to protect you," he continued, his eyes locking on mine. "Not because of the bond. Not because of duty. Because you—" His voice caught, roughened. "Because *you* are worth protecting. And because wanting you . . . it's not just my wolf. It's me. All of me."

The vulnerability in his face hit harder than any declaration. This was a man who had fought gods and shadows, who had bled and killed without hesitation, and here he was, telling me he desired something as simple, as impossible, as *me*.

Grief and gratitude warred in his expression, the lines of his face pulled taut like he wasn't sure which one would win. "I admire your strength. Your fire. You make me want things I never thought I'd have again. Things I never thought I'd want again. And it's—" His hands flexed at my waist, like he couldn't decide whether to pull me closer or let go before he broke something. "It's bringing me to my knees."

My wolf lunged forward in my chest, teeth bared in a feral grin. *Now,* she growled. *Now, before the world takes this from us again.* Her urgency bled into me, heat and need rising so fast I could barely think. All I knew was the feel of his hands, the scent of him wrapping around me, the bond between our wolves sparking.

I swallowed hard, my voice low, almost shaking. "Gabriel—"

His gaze dropped to my mouth, then back to my eyes. His wolf's presence pressed against mine, hungry, certain. And for the first time, I didn't want to hold anything back. Not the need. Not the bond. Not the part of me that had been aching for him since the moment he'd held me in the dream world.

"Do you want me?" he asked, his voice desperate.

"I've never wanted anyone more."

CHAPTER
THIRTY-SIX

ERIN

Gabriel didn't rush. He stood with me in the middle of the room, breathing me in, palms warm at my waist as if learning the exact breadth of me. His mouth found my temple first, a brush of heat that skimmed along my hairline. Another kiss at the corner of my eye. The slow reverence of it unraveled nerves one by one. His hands slid up my sides, fingers splaying over ribs, thumbs stroking the edge of my sternum like he'd mapped this path a thousand times and still needed to confirm every landmark.

"Tell me if I go too fast," he murmured against my cheek.

"Make me wait," I breathed, and the answer moved through him like a current.

A slow smile spread over his lips. "Learn something from Malachai?"

I blushed, and he greedily obeyed my request. He teased patience into a ritual.

Fabric rasped as he eased my shirt over my head, knuckles

grazing skin. Cool air kissed my bare shoulders, but heat followed where his mouth went next—collarbone, the hollow at the base of my throat, the line of my shoulder. He didn't claim. He coaxed. He made a worship out of restraint and a promise out of every inch he didn't take.

Yes, my wolf rumbled, pacing, tail high. *This. Ours.*

His buttons loosened under my fingers, and his breath hitched when I smoothed the leather from his shoulders. Scars bracketed muscle and old strength. He stood steady while I pushed the straps down his arms, his eyes never leaving mine.

The couch caught the backs of my knees. He guided me down, not to pin but to frame, one hand braced beside my head, the other cradling my jaw. The first real kiss had no urgency in it. He shaped it, tasted once, again, then deeper, tongue sliding slowly until my lungs forgot their job and my body remembered what it had been built to answer.

Heat climbed under my skin, sweet and inexorable. He drew back only to look—gaze heavy, lashes low—and then he kissed the corner of my mouth. His teeth grazed my lower lip. A small, involuntary sound slipped free, and his answering hum vibrated through his chest and into mine.

"I never thought I'd do this again," he rasped.

"I never thought I'd find a mate."

He chuckled at that, then worked to remove my clothes in increments. He pulled on my zipper. I unbuckled his belt. He chucked off my denim with a firm tug and a laugh caught between us when my heel snagged. His patience never cracked. He pressed kisses to my knees while he worked the fabric down, to my ankle as he freed it, to the inside of my calf like he had all the time in the world to ruin me.

"Look at me," he said, and when I did, something in him softened and broke open. Gratitude. Grief. Want. All of it bared.

He came over me, the weight of him settling into the cradle

of my hips, the warm slide of skin against skin where nothing separated us anymore. The scent of him deepened, cedar, smoke, clean sweat, the edge of wild that lived under his control. He dragged his mouth down my throat, lingering over my pulse, and my wolf pressed closer, ears flat with pleasure.

"Let me," he whispered, and then he took his time teaching me the language he'd wanted to speak when I'd been under Malachai's eyes. He mouthed the slope of my breast, the curve beneath, the peaked sensitivity he teased with deliberate patience until the ache gathered and broke and gathered again. His hand held my hip steady as his tongue wrote over skin. His other hand anchored me by our joined fingers, knuckles brushing the couch fabric, thumb tracing circles that said stay with me, *stay, stay.*

My breath shortened, my knees fell wider. Every nerve learned a new name. He read each change like a map: the catch when his thumb swept lower, the shiver at the line where my thigh met my torso, the way my spine arched when he kissed just beneath my ribs. He didn't press past any gate he hadn't opened on purpose.

"Please," slipped out, unguarded. "Please, Gabriel."

He stilled for a heartbeat, forehead touching mine, chest rising hard. "Pleasure with no fear. No bargains. Only us."

"Only us."

He slid a hand under my thigh and hitched me closer, slow enough that the world narrowed to the burn and the give. Our joining stole thought. He waited, breath a ragged measure against my mouth. My body opened, the stretch turned to fullness, to rightness, to the kind of relief that feels like coming up from deep water and breaking surface into air.

He moved, measured, steady as a promise. Hips rolled, withdrew, returned, each movement a tease that pulled sound from my throat and a growl from my wolf. He watched my face while he took me apart, adjusting angle and depth until sensation sparked bright and sure along every wire inside me.

As he dropped his chest to mine, a memory flooded my head. Torches guttering in a stone room, his back against the wall and my skirts shoved up around my hips as laughter turned to gasps. Wheat bending around us in a summer field as we lay together hidden from the world. A tent at winter's edge, canvas snapping with wind while his mouth warmed every place the cold had claimed.

The nights we'd been torn apart by duty. The mornings we'd found our way back to skin and breath and the simple miracle of our bond. Pain flickered in the oldest of them and, as our bodies found the rhythm that always belonged to us, that pain knit closed. Thread by thread, those lost pieces stitched into the present until there was no space between then and now.

Mine, my wolf exulted. *All of him, all of me. Now.*

He groaned, low and helpless, when the bond flared. It lit behind my breastbone like the first spark catching tinder—tiny, then leaping, then roaring across everything we were. Our wolves rushed into it, meeting mid-leap. Heat flashed through every nerve, through marrow, through the places language couldn't name. I tightened around him, he answered with a thrust that drew the air from my lungs.

"Erin." His voice broke on my name, and then he let the control go. Pleasure pulled tight. He held my gaze as the bond locked with a click, a flare, and belonging slammed home so hard my eyes stung. The mating bond snapped into place with a rush of wild joy that shook my bones.

I crested, nails biting his shoulders, mouth open against his jaw as sound tore out of me. Release scanned every inch of me and rewrote it, heat flooding down and back up, pulsing around him. He followed with a ragged groan and a shudder I felt everywhere we touched, sinking deeper, bracing, releasing.

We clutched at each other, jerky and desperate, then stilled, breath heaving, foreheads pressed together. The world narrowed to heartbeat and warmth and the murmuring hum of a bond that would not dim. He kissed me once, slow as the first, then took my hand in his and turned my wrist up to the light.

"Here. Because nobody gets to taste your blood. Nobody but me." His teeth grazed the tender skin on the inside, exactly where my pulse beat.

The bite was quick, precise, claiming and gentle all at once. Heat rolled under my skin as the mark took—no pain, only the deep rightness of being named by the one I had chosen. His tongue soothed the sting, sealing it with warmth. A cool breath skimmed the damp, and the bond answered, thrumming content.

I dragged him closer again because distance suddenly felt like hunger. "Don't ever stop guarding me."

"Never," he said, and the word settled over my skin. "You saved me."

"We saved each other."

He sighed deeply. "I love you."

"I love you," I whispered back as my eyes dropped closed.

My wolf curled down, satisfied. A queen on her throne.

THIRTY-SEVEN

ERIN

Rowan's shop glowed like a hearth against the October gray. Strings of amber bulbs looped over the ceiling beams, casting coins of light across oil-dark floors and the long counter Rowan had sanded by hand. Coffee steamed in mismatched mugs. Evelyn had tucked spruce tips and tiny white pumpkins along the shelves between carburetors and jars of bolts, a marriage of grease and grace that felt exactly like our lives.

The bell over the door chimed, and cold air threaded in around us. Connor and Mia walked in carrying a tray of cookies. Kael and Callista leaned over a chessboard near the window, but Kael happily left the game to be the first to sample.

Destin had claimed the broad arm of a leather chair, knee bouncing, Lana draped sideways across the rest of him. Liam and Tori bickered cheerfully at the snack table about whether ketchup belonged on anything in this province. Connor stood with his back to the wall, protective even at a party, one hand at the small of Mia's back.

Gabriel's fingers brushed the inside of my wrist, then tugged on the cord of the amulet. We'd found it in the woods along with the other relics, now just ordinary objects. I gave the dagger to Lana, but the other three were still up for grabs. Nobody had claimed them yet. I couldn't blame them.

"Okay, okay," Rowan called, rapping a spoon against a metal tray until the sound cut through the clatter. He stood behind the counter like a ringmaster, grease on his knuckles, eyes bright. Evelyn slipped beside him, hand tucked in his elbow. Her cheeks carried that fresh-from-the-wind flush she never lost, but tonight she glowed in a way that had nothing to do with weather or the warm bulbs overhead.

"We said this was a shop-warming," Rowan began, grin twitching, "because the windows are finally replaced and Kael swears the new filter will keep the coffee from tasting like dog shit."

"I've tested it. It works," Kael said proudly, grabbing another cookie.

"But," Rowan continued, "we lied."

Evelyn's fingers tightened on his arm. Her smile went soft and brave. "We asked you here because we wanted all of you in the same room when we told you."

Silence landed, heavy and expectant. Even Liam stopped chewing.

"We're having a pup," Rowan said.

The room detonated. Destin whooped, that deep-barrel noise that rattled the glass in the display case. Lana's face split into a grin so wide it should have scared small gods. Connor's hand left Mia's back so he could clap Rowan's shoulder hard enough that the man winced and laughed at the same time.

Tori launched herself around the counter to crush Evelyn in a hug that made her squeak. Kael lifted a brow at Callista, and her eyes grew bright with tears. Even Brama, lurking near the door with Ansel, let a rare smile loosen his stern mouth.

"And," Callista stood, her voice nervous. "since we're apparently doing announcements . . . we're having one too."

Kael's eyes flew wide. Destin almost fell off the arm of the chair. Mia shrieked. I crashed into Callista, and we both laughed into each other's shoulders until the world steadied. Kael cleared his throat and tried for dignified, failed, then snatched Callista from between us and whirled her around.

Rowan wiped at his eyes, tried to compose himself. "Family. That's the word."

Lana lifted her mug. "To what we burned," she said, and didn't wince when the room sobered. "And what we built after."

We drank. Coffee, tea, water, whatever. It didn't matter.

"What's restored," Tori added, sliding a fresh tray of sausage rolls on the counter, "stays ours. Wards. Territory. The fact that I can sleep a whole night without waking to check the perimeter cams."

Everyone chuckled.

"The borders are safe. Our humans are safe," Connor said.

Malachai's vampires were gone. Connor had gone up and checked himself.

Lana leaned back against him, head on his shoulder. "The wards will hold. Evelyn and I scrubbed every thread. Tied them to what actually lasts. Pack bonds."

"More powerful than any relic," Evelyn said, one hand sweeping as if she could gather all of us into her fingers. "We don't need to own power. We only need each other."

That line lodged under my ribs like a blessing. For months, power had been all I could smell, think, dream. The heat of it, the fear of it. It had stolen from me, tried to rewire my heart. And now, standing in warm shop-light, I understood what a pack was supposed to be. Not a fortress. A net. The kind you cast together over cold dark water, so when anyone goes under, there are twenty hands hauling them back out.

Mia's gaze snagged on my wrist, and she flipped it over. The mark glowed faintly, heat under skin. A small amulet stared up at her.

"Erin," she whispered, and then louder, laughing through tears. "It's beautiful." Her arms locked around my neck, breath warm in my hair. "You deserve it," she said into my ear. "You both do. About time the world gave you one thing without a knife in it."

Gabriel's hand found my lower back as if drawn by a magnet, anchoring, steady. Gratitude surged so hard my knees loosened. He didn't step forward to be congratulated or slapped on the back. He simply stood at my spine like he had decided that was his post and no one would argue him off it.

"Welcome to the mated-people club." Callista grinned at Kael. "Dues are steep. Benefits are worth it."

Liam leaned on the counter. "Don't rub it in. Someone needs to find me a woman."

Tori raised an eyebrow, and Liam flushed pink. He cleared his throat. "So are we doing Halloween or what? I'm not letting Kael spend the whole party reading a baby book and pretending it's a grimoire."

Kael sniffed. "It's never too early to study. And if I dress as a wizard, what then?"

"Then you'd still scare the kids," Destin deadpanned.

Evelyn sighed. "Pumpkin walk on the trail. Hot cider. Costume contest. Crafts in the bay." She pointed toward the roll-up door where Rowan kept the old Land Cruiser. "Mia, you can judge the cutest pup."

"I'm thinking lumberjack," Liam said.

"Firefighter," Connor jumped in.

Mia rolled her eyes. "C'mon. Stretch yourself."

"Fine. Sexy lumberjack," Liam said, and Tori smacked his arm with a tea towel.

Brama's voice slid in from the door, quieter, older. "You stand in a circle and speak of holidays," he said. "For a long time, we only spoke of campaigns. This is better."

Ansel nodded once, long mouth curved in something that might have been contentment.

Gabriel's thumb traced the edge of my mark, just once. Heat rippled out from the point of contact, bond answering like a plucked string. *Home,* my wolf hummed, and the word didn't mean a place. It meant this. Fluorescent lights. Too few chairs. Cookies on a plate, and laughter.

I leaned my shoulder into Gabriel's chest and let the whole ordinary, extraordinary scene soak in. The ache that had owned me for months eased. The quiet inside me wasn't the absence of fear. It was the presence of everything else.

The bell chimed as someone new nosed in—a neighbor, curious. An elder who got word of cookies. A kid who wanted to see the inside of a car engine.

Tori clapped her hands once to call attention back. "Costumes," she declared. "Group theme. No arguments."

Liam lifted both palms in surrender. "All right. Twist my arm."

Rowan raised a brow. "And the theme?"

Tori grinned, wicked and wild. "Please. Like you had to ask."

Wolves. It had to be wolves.

Join my Substack to read every new book FIRST before it's published.

Look for "The Brothers Kade"
Coming soon...

Have you read "I Won't Date the Wolf Prince"? What Happens on the Island Stays on the Island...

ALSO BY LUNA M. ROSE

WILD FATED
SHADOW PACK LEGENDS
LUNA M. ROSE

SHADOW PACK LEGENDS
FIRE FATED
LUNA M. ROSE

BLOOD FATED
SHADOW PACK LEGENDS
LUNA M. ROSE

I WON'T
DATE
THE
WOLF
PRINCE
WOLF ISLAND: SEASON 1
LUNA M. ROSE

About the Author

Luna masquerades as a well-adjusted, functioning adult, but she secretly still believes in magic and wild things hidden just beyond the veil of our world. She has a fairy garden (with lights!) and lives with her husband and children near the Rocky Mountains in Colorado. She adores shiny objects.

9 781955 286831